10726236

COPYRIGHT

Copyright © 2022 TL Shively. All Rights Reserved worldwide. No part of this document may be reproduced or transmitted in any form, by any means, including photocopying, recording, or other electronic or mechanical methods, without prior written permission from the author, except for brief quotations embodied in critical reviews and certain other noncommercial uses permitted by copyright law. Author retains 100% of the rights and copyright licenses to the manuscript and all other materials submitted.

Disclaimer: The publisher has put forth its best efforts in preparing and arranging this eBook and printed book. The information provided herein by the author is provided "as is" and you read and use this information at your own risk. The publisher and author disclaim any liabilities for any loss of profit or commercial or personal damages resulting from the use of the information contained in this eBook and printed book.
ISBN: 978-1-952325-11-3

Edited by: Partners In Crime Book Services
Formatting by: Rebecca Poole of Dreams2media

HAVEN'S SHADOW

GUARDIANS OF SANCTUARY BOOK 5

TL SHIVELY

ACKNOWLEDGEMENTS

I would like to thank all my readers, family and friends that have supported me along my journey to bring my imagination to life. And to those select few who find themselves starring between the pages of my books, thank you for putting your fictional lives in my hands.

OTHER BOOKS BY AUTHOR

SANCTUARY GUARDIAN SERIES READING ORDER:
The Secret Sanctuary
The Town That Time Forgot
The Battle of Sleeping Lady
The Independence Mine Disaster
Hunter's Betrayal
Haven's Shadow

SPIDER'S TRILOGY
Spider's Awakening

ALSO FROM AUTHOR:
Sanctuary and Friends coloring book

CHAPTER 1

The air at the Wolf Den where Telara and Pam enjoyed lunch was tense as students were sitting with books, laptops and papers on the tables as they ate. One more week of school left, then they would be free for the summer. It had only been two years ago that Telara, Tia, Vanna, Cole, Chad, Chance and I.Q. went to Sanctuary where they met Pam and all their new friends, but to Telara it felt as if they had always been friends.

The irony of that was their first meeting was not the friendliest, nor their second, Telara thought grimly. They had come to Sanctuary only to discover they were the Guardians of Sanctuary, which meant they were the only descendants of the Gods or Goddesses that were granted physical power. Tia had the power of wind, Vanna was gifted with the power of Mother Nature herself, I.Q. was granted the power of electricity, Cole had the power of fire, Chad had the power of ice, while his brother had the power of water, and Telara was cursed with the power of the mind.

Pretty cool huh? Except the past Guardians made a reputation for being vain and unfriendly. Something that created a large hurdle for the current Guardians to get over. It took losing a mutual friend and two of the hardest heads in Sanctuary to put their egos in check, mainly her and Pam. After that, they became friends, something that had only grown stronger during their adventures.

Pam even took it upon herself to help them find a way so they might live past the prophecy. Yeah, real cool powers came with an ominous prophecy that told of their deaths as well. Guardians were born that would train until they could take on the Shadow Master and his Magine, then a great battle would ensue that would end the Guardians' lives. The best part is that even after they gave their lives, the Magine would rise again and the next set of Guardians would be born. Stupid prophecies.

Although, as Gage, Pam's second in the Alpha Faction back at Sanctuary and their new "gym teacher" at school, pointed out, they already changed the prophecy. They are the first Guardians to ever work with any of the Factions at Sanctuary, they are the first Guardians to live with their families instead of at Sanctuary, they are the first Guardians to ever visit any of the other Sanctuaries or their outposts, and the biggest difference is they are the first Guardians to have friends.

"You will be a senior next year," Pam's words pulled Telara from her musings and it took her a moment or two before the words registered, when they did she chuckled. They were heading to their hideout where the others were waiting for them. I.Q.'s tone of voice carried an urgency that no one could ignore, he wasn't one to get dramatic and when he said it was urgent, they listened.

"Yeah, I will." Telara acknowledged then with a smirk she asked, "so, when did you graduate?" They had all been playing the games of trying to figure out the ages of their Arion friends. Something that no one seemed inclined to let spill. From the little tidbits they gathered throughout the past few years they learned that the Arions were born in Sanctuary, everything they learned, they learned in Sanctuary. Some stayed and made their lives there while others might transfer to another branch of Sanctuary. Seemed almost every day they were learning something new.

Pam kept walking staring straight although she did brush an errant dark lock of hair that had dared to fall from her ponytail, away from her face, "next year, right alongside you and everyone else."

For a moment Telara was confused about her remark but when she remembered her question she groaned, "you know what I mean." After returning from the Rouge Hunter's underground town last summer, they had to do some fancy talking to get their parents on board with them getting their licenses. Cole had to do some extra work at his parent's bakery to prove he could be mature enough; Tia didn't believe it helped much. One time when they went to pick him up, they found him singing with the mop that was dripping dirty water all over the floor.

Somehow, they managed to get through their driver's ed schooling, getting the drive time done in between school work as well as training until they finally had their licenses. Their restricted licenses but still their licenses. Still, they walked wherever they went; the only one with a car was Vanna and she liked the walking. Said it made her feel closer to nature rather than driving by like a blur.

The past year it seemed they were doing anything they could to avoid discussing what had happened in Illinois, Flint's name never came up and they didn't talk about the fact there was more that was being hidden from them. They lived as normally as they could, trained with Pam and the other Arions on different fighting techniques as well as using their Crims. They would practice their powers to the best of their abilities but they always felt as if they were lacking in that area.

It wasn't only Pam who was helping them try to stay alive, the other Arions were helping with digging to see if there was any prophecy or information that could tell them how to avoid dying when they came up against the Magine, something that was getting closer and closer each day. Something else they tried not to bring up. Flint's words would come back to her about how the Shadow Master didn't want to hurt them, she really wanted to believe that but history doesn't lie.

Zach was no help, she would ask him if he knew anything about the Shadow Master and he would give her that small smile of his, the one that said he wished he could give her the answers she wanted but he couldn't. His visits started to slow down when she would press so she stopped asking, instead they would talk about her training, schooling and what idiot things Cole and Chad had done that day.

Ignore, suppress and repeat had become their motto.

"I.Q. didn't give any clue as to what he wanted to talk to us about?" Pam asked as she moved from the street, stepping over the curb as they moved into the woods that surrounded their hideout. Good thing they were wearing walking shoes, Tia would be wearing the ankle boots she loved so much and those heels would be sinking into the soft ground that still hadn't completely dried from the Michigan spring.

Telara moved her shoulder in a dismissive manner. "Nope, just that we needed to see what he had found."

Moving off the path they had been walking through the woods, they stepped out onto the lawn of the hideout, overgrown so as to keep up with the illusion that the house was abandoned. Making sure to avoid groundhog tunnels dug into the ground and tree limbs that had fallen, they made it to the rickety steps. Opening the door they moved through the house, hearing the murmuring from downstairs the closer they got to the basement door.

"Sounds like we're the last ones here," Pam said as she moved around one of the fallen chairs that littered the hallway. Opening the door, they started down the stairs and with the first creak, the murmuring stopped. Pam looked back at Telara with raised brows, Telara just shrugged both her shoulders moving forward. She wasn't sure why her friends had stopped talking when they heard them but the only way to find out was to see what was going on.

The TV that usually sat in front of the couch was pushed off into a corner and in its place were some blackboards on easels, I.Q. was sitting in a high back lazy boy that Vanna's parents were tossing out last fall situated on the other side of the couch, a long oak coffee table in between. Vanna and Tia were seated on the couch with solemn looks as they looked up at them. Cole was lounging in the oversized armchair while Chad was seated in a folding chair and his brother was seated on a beanbag on the floor. All wearing the same solemn expression of Vanna and Tia, staring at them.

Telara sighed. "Just spill it."

I.Q. looked over at Tia who nodded making Telara wonder if she really wanted to know, the solemn looks they gave when her and Pam entered the room had set her arm hairs standing on end but the look I.Q. had given Tia had the butterflies doing the mamba in her stomach. I.Q. turned the stargazer around so that they could see the screen, she hadn't realized that it was on the table until he had done that but the biggest shock was the face staring out at her from the screen.

Hers.

"Where…" she started to say as she looked at the pic, nothing about it looked familiar to her. She couldn't remember it ever being taken; the outfit was nothing she had ever seen before either. Like something from a fantasy movie or maybe a renaissance festival with the leather and scaly look. "Is that Ra?" Her nose crinkled as she squinted at the picture. "I know that isn't me but I don't think Ra would ever wear that, no designer label. Wait a minute!" Her back straightened up, "That's the Stargazer. How is a picture of someone that looks like me in the Stargazer?" She looked at I.Q., confusion swimming in her eyes.

"Now you see why I said you needed to come and see what I had found. I was doing some more translating and this picture appeared," I.Q. told her.

"What were you translating when it appeared?" Pam asked.

"Looking for other Paladins," I.Q. told her.

"So, is that a Paladin?" Telara felt as if she was floating out to sea with no land in sight.

"We don't know." Tia looked up at her from her

seated position. "I.Q. was having a problem looking up the other Paladins so he started typing in random names and that picture came up."

"We didn't want to take the chance of losing the picture before you could see it by looking anything else up, I wasn't sure I would be able to get back to the picture," I.Q. told her looking back down at the Stargazer and the picture of the person who looked an awful lot like her. "I had opened an entry that spoke of other Paladins but not by name, I got testy when I started just typing in random names." He gave a chagrined shrug. "Wish I knew more about this." He gave a helpless gesture towards the Stargazer.

"You are the smartest one here," Vanna assured him. "None of the rest of us could have even figured out how to turn it on; if anyone here is going to do it, it's going to be you."

"The symbols are easy enough to figure out," he told her. "Every language has a common universal basis you can base your translations on; when you figure out the base the rest falls into place."

"Except, even you admitted you had never seen that language whether in ancient times nor current days," Chance reminded him. "That is a language no one has seen and you translated it."

"Not all of it." I.Q. snorted.

"Not yet." Van looked over at him with confidence.

"Maybe this person is a past Guardian," Pam mused.

Cole sat up straight. "Hey, that could be. They are our ancestors, it would make sense that one of them resembled one of us." His eyes went bright. "I wonder if there is one that looks like me."

Tia rolled her eyes so hard Telara thought she could almost hear it. "No one could be that cruel."

Cole frowned at her and Telara bit back a grin, even in the direst of moments they could find something to bicker about, like an old married couple. Looking back at the picture she gave a deep sigh.

Pam looked over at her. "What's wrong?"

"Just not sure this is worth our time, honestly," Telara admitted.

"What do you mean, not worth our time?" Chance sat up straight in the bean bag. "Telly, she has your face, don't you want to know who she is?"

Telara gave a soft snort. "Of course I do, but we're supposed to be looking for anything to help us in defeating the Magine without dying." She gave a helpless gesture towards the Stargazer. "This feels more like a personal inquiry rather than one of necessity."

"I wouldn't say that," Pam told her, staring at the picture as well.

Telara turned quickly looking at her with a surprised look, she was sure out of all of them here, Pam would agree with her. "Why do you say that?"

Pam looked back at her. "We were told that we needed to find out the true history if we wanted to keep history from repeating itself." Everyone nodded, they remembered Soliel's words in Alaska. Pam looked back at the picture of the golden haired Telara lookalike with those same blue eyes. "Seems to me, she is history and could possibly hold the key to revealing everything we need."

"Or she could be a dead end," Telara countered.

Pam looked at her. "Only one way to find out."

"After exams," I.Q. iterated to which Cole, Chad and even Chance groaned.

"He's right." Pam nodded to their evident displeasure.

"We're old enough to fight Shadows and possibly die trying to save the world and we still have to take exams," Cole muttered with a dark look.

Telara gave a sympathetic look. "It doesn't seem fair but we all voted to live normal lives and for Juniors the last week is exams."

"Don't forget Senior pictures," Tia's eyes lit up. "I got a special wardrobe I can't wait to showcase."

Laughter filled the room and after a grumbling or two, they agreed that after exams and pictures they would start investigating this new development.

"Telara, I want you and Tiara on the bridge over here," her mother called to her, shielding her eyes with her hand as she shouted to Telara, who had stopped when a flash of bright light caught her attention.

Not seeing anything, she fought back the urge to go investigate, which would probably have her mother sending her father or brother, who was home visiting, after her. Her mother and sister were standing by the bridge, the light shining off their blond hair as her mother situated Tiara where she wanted her for the photographer who was talking to her dad and brother.

"Hey kiddo." Her brother pulled her into his muscular arms as she neared them, they had always been close growing up. She was proud of him when he went into the military but really missed him. He had the dark looks of their father but his bright blue eyes mirrored hers as she grinned up at him.

"Steve, let your sister go so I can get this shot done please." Her mother stood there with her hands on her hips, staring at them with an indulgent look. Tiara was standing behind her, her lips twitching. Growing up Telara and Steve had done their fair share of causing or creating trouble while Tiara would watch and sometimes join in.

Her brother was very athletic as well as fun loving, he had always been popular in school without even trying. Her sister was on the cheer squad, her clothes all of designer labels, and then there was Telara, the awkward one in the bunch who never had a specialty until she came to Sanctuary, where she learned how to fight Shadows and levitate things.

Telara gave her brother a final squeeze and moved down to where her mother and sister were waiting. Her sister was dressed casually in a light blue off the shoulder short outfit while Telara was dressed in ripped jeans, which was the style, as well as a white cotton top and a short blue cardigan. Her mother had convinced her to forgo her running shoes that was her staple and wear a pair of brown suede dress boots while her sister was wearing white leather sandals. These outfits were probably the ninth or tenth time they had changed. Their brother was lucky, he had one outfit that he wore the whole time since their mother hadn't insisted he bring multiple outfits with him.

After they finished this pose, which was supposed to be the last one, her mother spoke with the photographer with Tiara, Steve and her dad standing off to the side. Telara decided to use this time to see if she could discover where that flash of light had come from.

Walking away from her family she moved across one of the many stone bridges in this park that were sculpted to look like wooden bridges over different parts of the stream that ran through this park. Past some of the towering trees in this park, but none as tall as the elder tree in Sanctuary, there was a large bird house that could house hundreds of birds.

Another flash had her moving over a hill past some bushes and coming to a complete stop. There before her, stood Flint, his lips curled into a smile she wasn't sure she wanted to trust.

"What are you doing here?" she demanded.

"I told you I would be keeping an eye on you," he said with a dismissive wave of his hand as if that explained everything.

"Yeah, that doesn't sound at all creepy," Telara grunted sarcastically, glaring at him.

Flint ignored her sarcasm and looked over to where her family stood talking with the photographer who was packing up all his equipment, he remarked, "You two are identical."

Telara didn't even fight the eyeroll. "Identical twins usually are."

"You're the prettier one, more natural," he mused, still looking over at her family.

"Identical twins," Telara reminded him with an exasperated posture.

"True," he acknowledged with amusement. "But I can tell the difference."

"Whatever." Telara dismissed the entire subject with one word before going on the attack. "What do you want?"

"Was wondering if you changed your mind?" His gaze moved from her family back to her.

"Join you and that psychopath you are working for who wants to destroy all magic and do unspeakable things to the world we live in?" She crossed her arms staring at him. "Not a cold day in Hades."

"Everyone has their own perceptions, personally I was just tired of being lied to by people who didn't care two cents about me," he said, looking around him. "This is a nice park, Stazi would love this place."

"She might," Telara agreed. "But I bet she wouldn't want you with her anymore."

He looked back at her. "I bet she would." His voice, so full of confidence, grated across her nerves.

"You know what, I don't need this aggravation, this was a family occasion and you weren't invited," Telara turned to leave but Flint reached out and grabbed her arm.

"Wait!"

She took a deep breath and turned around giving him one of her exasperated looks. "What?" She spoke very sharp in clipped tones.

"Would you give Pam something for me?" he asked.

She frowned, "I'm not your messenger."

"Please, she won't talk to me."

Telara stared at him in disbelief. "Are you mental? You work for the bad guy!"

"That is the Sanctuary talking."

"No," Telara said, her whole body tightening with the aggravation she felt building. "This is me talking, you know, one of the Guardians your boss wants to kill!" She glared at him.

"I told you, he doesn't want your death." Flint sounded exasperated with her.

"And the past Guardians?" she countered, not caring
if he was getting aggravated with her, she was already
aggravated with him.

Flint shrugged. "Ask him."

"I would rather vanquish him," she retorted.

Flint gave a slow shake of his head as if he was done
with this conversation and tossed her a small package
that she caught before it hit the ground. "Give it to my
sister or throw it away, up to you. If you do give it to her,
tell her I'm sorry it's late."

Telara looked down at the small brown package in
her hand then back up but Flint was already gone.

"Telara!"

She turned and jogged off to where her mother and
the others were looking for her.

"Let's go grab something to eat," her mother said
when she reached them.

Telara gave an absent nod, throwing one last look
over her shoulder where she and Flint had been talking.
Biting her lip, she slid the package into her cardigan
pocket.

CHAPTER 2

Not easy when your big brother leaves," Pam spoke behind Telara, who was sitting outside with her feet in their backyard in-ground pool. Pam took off her shoes and socks, taking a seat next to Telara she joined her, kicking her feet softly in the water. It's been two years since Pam came to their home as an exchange student, part of the ruse Sanctuary came up with to help them be able to live with their families. At the end of the year her parents received an offer to extend the program, which they did after minimal coercion from Telara. It seemed as if Sanctuary had a solution for everything.

Steve left that morning, deployed to Arizona before heading to California where his new position waited. He had been promoted and was excited to start this new chapter, but she already missed him.

Telara pressed her lips together, her hand absently going to the brown package that was in her jean short pocket. Pam had been at Sanctuary during the senior pictures, and when she had returned, they were having a farewell party for Steve, so Telara hadn't really had any private time to give her Flint's package. When they had managed to make it back to bed, they passed out.

"Speaking of brothers," Telara started, not looking at Pam, instead her gaze stayed on the pool water's surface. She felt Pam stiffen next to her, but she stayed silent. "Flint showed up at our senior pictures at the park."

She wasn't looking at Pam but could see her wavy expression in the pool's surface, and saw Pam blanch at her words. "Did you talk to him?" Telara nodded. "What did he have to say?"

"Said he had been watching me and asked if I had thought about his offer."

Pam snorted. "To become a traitor like him."

Telara gave a soft lift of her shoulders. "I told him no, of course. But that wasn't all he had to say."

This time Pam turned to look at her. "What do you mean?"

Telara turned to look at her. "He gave me something to give you." She pulled out the package and handed it to Pam, who took it after a slight hesitation, not that Telara could blame her. "He told me to tell you he was sorry it's late."

Pam looked down at the package silently.

"I'll give you some privacy," Telara started to rise from her position but Pam's steadying hand on her shoulder stayed her.

"No, we're in this together, please stay."

Telara settled back down and watched as Pam unwrapped the package slowly and then pulled out a heart with a piece missing silver charm. Telara noticed how Pam gave a hard swallow and her eyes started to shine bright with unshed tears. Feeling like an interloper, she had to fight down the urge to rise up and leave. Pam asked her to stay so she stayed.

"When Flint left Sanctuary to head up the Hunters with Stazi, he had given me a charm bracelet so that I would know he would always be there for me," Pam said as a single tear fell down her cheek. "Every year on my birthday he would send me a new charm to add to it." Wiping angrily at the single tear she closed her fist around the charm.

Telara thought about the collection of sand bottles her sister had on one of the many shelves in her room. Her brother would send them to her from each place he had been stationed or visited, labeled the small jars for her. In Telara's room, in her small curio cabinet was the collection of thimbles her brother had collected for her. It wasn't a birthday tradition or anything, just something their brother wanted them to have so they knew he was always thinking of them. It was something they both treasured dearly.

Pam put the charm in her pocket and rose, the water dripping from her calves onto the stone patio around the pool. "The rest of the Guardians are waiting at the hideout for us, we should get going." Telara said nothing as she stood up as well, this was something that wasn't any of her business and she valued Pam's friendship too much to keep pushing on something this touchy.

"About time you guys showed up," Cole spoke around the pizza he was chomping on, earning him a glare from Tia and even Vanna.

"Swallow, then speak." Tia shook her head then

looked at Pam and Telara looking concerned. "Everything okay?"

Pam nodded crisply. "Everything is fine, are we ready to head to Sanctuary?"

"Are there some records of past Guardians at Sanctuary we can look through?" I.Q. asked her as he packed up his stargazer and the ancient looking book into his bag.

"Better," Pam told him and laughed at the arch of his brow. To I.Q., nothing was better than records or books with knowledge in them, any type of knowledge. "Don't forget we have our very own history buff at Sanctuary."

"That's right!" Chance said. "What's his name…" Laughter filled the room at his attempt of looking knowledgeable.

"Zeke," Pam filled in for him with a smirk. "The one who helped us with Lapros."

"That's right." Chance held up his finger, giving it two smart jerks. "Just testing your memory." The finger went down quickly with the not so believing looks he was getting.

"Let's go talk with him instead of wasting our time here," Vanna stood and walked up the stairs, leaving them to follow or be left behind. I.Q. touched the frame after shutting the door, they saw an electrical current move around the door activating the unseen security system I.Q. created with crystals placed in strategic positions around the whole house. They headed up the rickety stairs to the upstairs and master bedroom situated in the back where they had another crystal set up. This one was a present Claw gave them, at the beginning of their junior year, it created what he called a crystal door that would transport them where they wished to go. Mostly Sanctuary, but Claw assured them it could take them elsewhere as well, although he did warn against saying anything to Ira.

"Lucius is looking for you," a dark-haired guy wearing a white coat told Pam as they passed him talking to another white coat in the hallways of Sanctuary as they headed to speak to Zeke in the Delta quarters.

Pam responded to him. "I'll make sure to see him before we leave, thanks Ben." Now, they knew why he looked so familiar, he was the one Vanna approached and asked his name last year.

They moved through the rest of the hallways without the notice of anyone else until they entered the Delta headquarters where Zeke was talking with a very imposing looking girl with dark black braids that cascaded down her back almost to her thighs. Hearing them approach both of them turned to greet them, well Zeke greeted them with a smile while she just stared at them with her dark piercing eyes. She towered over Zeke, who didn't seem a bit intimidated, they on the other hand, weren't so sure.

Zeke introduced them. "Guardians, meet my second, Amelia." Amelia inclined her head in their direction, the dark braids swinging with her movement. "She is my equal in all, tracking, research, you name it." They looked up at her in greeting but she had already turned away, heading out of the room.

"Unlike you," Pam told him, "she is one of few words."

Zeke gave a half unashamed shrug. "Another reason we work so well, she lets me do all the talking." Zeke joined in on the laughter at his comment. "So, what brings you here? And please don't try to insult my intelligence by saying you were just stopping in for a visit."

Pam took a deep breath. "We need some information on past Guardians."

Zeke's brow furrowed before he looked around them, then turned towards the stairway that led to the other levels in their headquarters. They followed him all the way to the third floor where there was only one crystal attached to the wall. With one touch, the wall opened before them, revealing a library that would make any librarian jealous. Had to be at least four stories of bookshelves lining the walls, not to mention several rows of bookshelves towering over them through the center of the room. Shiny wooden stairs led to each level, with wooden ladders on rollers to reach books just out of reach. Wooden tables with wooden chairs lined with red velvet as well as wooden couches with red velvet cushions.

"All this place is missing is a fireplace," Tia looked around her in wonder.

The sound of Zeke clearing his throat caught their attention, he pointed to a fireplace big enough to drive a van through in the center of the back wall. Fluffy cushions, rugs, chairs and tables with lamps on them were placed strategically around the fireplace to give someone a nice comfy place to read.

"Whoa," they breathed looking around them.

Think we will be able to get I.Q. out of here?

They tried to hide their grins at Cole's question.

I don't know about I.Q., Vanna came back. *But I'm thinking that I found my perfect vacation spot.*

They nodded in agreement with her as they joined Pam, who was seated at one of the many tables with Zeke who was watching at their reactions. "So, exactly what are you wanting to know?" he asked, leaning back in his chair.

"We were wondering exactly how much you knew about past Guardians?" Pam asked him.

"Very few know more than me, you know that." He said, his finger tapping on the table.

"I do." Pam agreed. "What about how they looked?"

Now he frowned. "What do you mean by that?"

"Are there any pictures of past Guardians?" Tia asked him, drawing his attention her way.

"Cameras weren't even invented during the last reign of Guardians." He shook his head. "The Guardian cycle runs about every three to four hundred years."

"Guardian cycle?" Tia looked around them. *Never heard it called that before.* Telara and the other Guardians gave covert shakes of their heads in agreement.

"That is what the historians of Sanctuary call it," Zeke explained to them. "There is an entire section on the six cycles of Guardians that were here before you guys and it is in this very library."

"Really?" Chad moved to the edge of his wooden chair, looking around him. "Where?"

Vanna put her hand on his "One thing at a time." He gave a disgruntled sigh before settling back into his seat.

"No pictures drawn or painted?" I.Q. asked Zeke, bringing the conversation back to pictures of the past Guardians.

Zeke looked over at his shelves with a thoughtful look on his face, then he rose and disappeared between the farthest row of bookshelves from them. He came back with a pile of books in his arms, he started handing them down the table. "If there is, they will be in one of these books." Sitting down, he started leafing through the book in front of him.

Several hours later they found a handful of drawn pictures but none that were very detailed, mostly they were just ink drawings that not even recognition software would be able to pick up. Telara closed the hardcover of the book she was looking through with a bit more force than necessary in her frustration and leaned back in her chair. "This is getting us nowhere."

"With no pictures in my books the one you should be talking to is Lucius," Zeke told them.

"Like he will tell us anything," Telara grumbled.

"Can't help with that," Zeke told them. "But hey, if you find anything let me know." He gestured to his shelves. "Can always use another journal."

Entering the bungalow, they had to admit there was the feeling of being home that they didn't even feel at the homes they had grown up in. Vanna ran her hands along the leaves of one of the potted plants who were starting to droop, and within seconds the plant came to life. A murmuring from the kitchen caught their attention so they started walking that way. As they got closer they could hear Lucius and some other voice that was vaguely familiar.

When they entered they saw the dark haired Lucius sitting there talking to a silver haired man. Lucius's hair still had the streaks of silver woven in his hair while his companion had streaks of dark hair woven within his silver. Even seated you could tell Lucius was the taller of the two, the other man was more stocky but both looked fit. They both wore buttoned printed shirts, jeans but while Lucius wore comfortable loafers the other man wore cowboy boots.

"Mark!" Cole said, excited that he could remember who the person was before the rest of them. After Cole said that, they realized that he was indeed Mark, the liaison from the Hunters' place.

"How are Stazi and Jeff doing?" Tia asked him.

"Good." He told her. "They have already taken care of all the structural damage that was done. The morale is another matter but they will get it done. They are a good team and they know what they're doing."

"You weren't expected to report back here for another two weeks, I thought you would choose to spend that time with family and friends," Lucius spoke up, watching them with a suspicious gleam.

Telara swiped her lips with her tongue to moisten them since they suddenly seemed to go dry before speaking, "Actually, we have a question for you."

A brow shot up, "for me?" She nodded. "Well, then, proceed." Lucius leaned back in his chair, his suspicious gleam turning to interest.

Telara thought about how to phrase the question that she wanted to ask but when Lucius tilted his head, all the thoughts of being sly about it flew right out of her head as she blurted out, "Were there any past Guardians that looked like me?"

Never before had they seen that many expressions cross his face, his curious expression tightened and they saw a brightness in his eyes as if he was tearing up but then all expression was gone as his expression went blank. "Why are you asking?"

Chewing on her bottom lip she looked at the others whose expressions became guarded, she had been about to tell him about the picture in the Stargazer but they realized they had never told him about the Stargazer.

"Something my brother said," Pam spoke up quickly.

Lucius gave her a look that showed he wasn't buying her sudden explanation and his response wasn't very encouraging at all, "with no pictures of past Guardians it would be near impossible to say," he told them then turned to Pam, "and your presence has been requested by the leadership of Haven, they are needing some assistance with training as well as protocols."

"My assistance?" Pam asked, her brow furrowing. "In Georgia?"

"They specifically asked for you." Lucius stared at her. "Any idea on why they would ask for you specifically?"

Pam's expression showed her confusion. "No clue."

"Well, regardless, they are asking for your assistance and the Leaders have approved their request so you need to pack a bag," Lucius told her, taking a sip from the blue ceramic looking coffee cup that they didn't notice sitting in front of him.

"What about us?" I.Q. asked, leaning back against the counter.

"Gage will take over your training until Pam returns," Lucius told him. "You can find him in Thetis having lunch with Claw, I believe."

"You know," Mark spoke up, grabbing all their attention, Lucius looked at him suspiciously. "I do think that outpost has someone there that knows almost as much as Lucius when it comes to past Guardians, possibly more." He sipped his drink from his silver metal cup, seemingly oblivious to the narrowed gaze Lucious threw his way.

"They need training," Lucius told him, his irritation showing in his voice. "Not running around on a field trip."

Mark looked up from his cup. "That sounds more like Ira than you."

Lucius said nothing but gave Mark a hard stare.

"We still have two weeks left before we're expected for training." I.Q pointed out while the others grinned in agreement, completely ignoring the tense undercurrent emanating from the two in front of them.

"Georgia sounds like a great vacation spot," Chance interjected.

Looking at Lucius, Telara could see that he wasn't amused with the turn of things, something about that seemed off to her. It was always Ira who pushed their training and not wanting them to leave Sanctuary, just as Mark had pointed out. Lucius never seemed to interfere but this time it was as if he didn't want them in Georgia, which made her want to go there.

"So, it's decided then." Mark spoke up, a gleam in his eye that spoke of a mischievous manner. "Have a nice trip and don't forget to bring me back a souvenir."

CHAPTER 3

Only Mark and Lucius remained in the kitchen, Lucius staring at the open doorway everyone had left through. "So, what are you up to?" Lucius asked, giving Mark a suspicious look while he kept sipping his drink.

"Who said I was up to something?"

"The innocent act doesn't work," Lucius told him dryly.

Mark shrugged. "Let's just say that their trip to Georgia is written in the stars."

Lucius sighed. "I thought you were the normal one.

Mark threw back his head and laughed. "Compared to the rest, I am."

"Not a comforting response," was the dry response from Lucius. "Why is it that I have to keep my obligations but you and the others can do as they please?"

Mark shrugged again. "I'm not under the same obligations as you, as a matter of fact, I am under NO obligations. They're smart kids and I believe they're the ones who've been foretold, all they need is a gentle push into the right direction."

Lucius didn't respond, just stared into his cup. "So, what is waiting for them in Georgia?"

"You can't protect them from their destiny," Mark told him gently. "Everyone wants them to make the right decisions but they don't want them to make their own choices. Right choices don't mean a thing when there is only one choice to make."

Lucius leaned his head back with a sigh. "You're right."

"Of course, I am." Mark looked at his watch. "Your problem is you are afraid of history repeating itself and you won't be able to save them again."

Lucius didn't respond but his pallor whitened as his hands tightened around his coffee cup.

"You can't take the weight of the world on your shoulder, my friend." Mark watched him. "You've been waiting for them to come back, to make things right. Now, you need to trust that they can do what they were meant to do."

Lucius looked up at him. "What if they aren't the ones, what if they don't survive?"

Mark leaned back in his chair, one hand resting on his own thigh while the other rested on the table holding his cup, "then we start over but you know as well as I do that, they are the ones, they even found your pictures that you encrypted. The other Guardians of the past had barely gotten past your first journal entry, hell, some never even bothered to open your journal."

"I know you're right," Lucius admitted. "I just wish I could be of more help to them, I hate hiding things that could help them."

"You know the consequences."

"What if I don't care?" Lucius countered. "They aren't just Guardians, they're family."

Mark nodded in agreement. "We know this, this isn't easy for everyone but there is a reason behind each decision made."

"Do you even know the reasons?" Lucius asked, leaning forward on the table.

"I'm not meant to," was Mark's simple response.

"And you are good with that?" Lucius asked him. "How can you accept orders without knowing the reason behind them?"

"I trust in something greater than me." Mark rose from the table. "You should try it sometime," with that he was gone leaving a disgruntled looking Lucius.

"Doesn't mean those who believe they are greater than us can't be wrong," Lucius spoke to the air.

"Aren't we going the wrong way?" Cole looked over his right shoulder to the path that leads to the command center, as they followed Pam past Fairy Fields with all its colorful flowers blooming and the fairies flitting through the air. A flash of blue was their only warning that Flash had come to say hi, Telara bit her bottom lip when I.Q. flinched.

"Haven isn't connected to the transports in the Command Center," Pam explained as they moved past the Fairy Fields and into the Sprite's Domain.

Flash wrinkled her nose at the deadened foliage around them before taking her leave, flying back into her lush home. Off in the distance they could see the Elder tree as it loomed over all Sanctuary. Moving through the trees they hear shouting with the sound of clay breaking.

"Sounds like the Harlick brothers are at it again?" Chance grinned while the others shook their heads, trudging on.

"Watch out!" Tia yanked Chance back just in time.

"Yippee-Ki-Aye!" A flash of red flew past them as Fritz rode through Sprite's Domain in his toy car, weaving through the dead trees and roots with the ease of a professional NASCAR driver.

"One of these days, someone is going to step on that dang car and break it," Chance grumbled.

"Someone did." Pam gave a rueful shake of her head. "They ended up leaving Sanctuary because their room was always bug infested and no matter how many times it was fumigated, they would always come back."

"In other words," Tia told him, "you should be thanking me."

"Thank you," Chance said, moving forward but making sure to keep an eye out for an errant sprite and his toy car."

From their left they could hear the sounds of Thetis, noise from the Cantina as well as the general populace going about their business. The Graeae sisters arguing over their eye, the sounds of mothers chastising their children for playing around the feet of Talos, the Guardian of Thetis. Those sounds were something they missed every time they went home.

"Who would've thought we would miss gnomes fighting over sisters and sisters fighting over their eyes?"

Each of the Guardians looked at each other; Cole's words were spot on which made them even more hilarious.

"Whoa!"

They stopped at I.Q.'s words. They had passed the village of Thetis several moments ago and were heading into territory they had never ventured into before. The sound of running water could be heard in the distance but their gazes were all on the line of trees before them. They were nothing like the tall trees in the Fable Forest, the smaller leafy ones in the Fairy Fields or even the deadened ones that litter the Sprite's Domain. The trunks of all the trees seemed intertwined with one another, so much that there were no passageways through them. It was like a wall of weaving branches with accents of leaves and other foliage creating a decorative canvas that loomed before them.

Pam turned around at the border of the trees, not that she could've gone much further with the wall of bark and limbs in front of her.

I.Q. glanced around them before letting his gaze fall on Pam. "So, what now? This feels very anticlimactic."

"Have to agree with I.Q. on this one," Chance looked around them. "Expecting something big and showy and all I see is a wall of wood. Can't even enter the forest let alone transport from here to Georgia."

"Unless, maybe we're already in Georgia," Tia suggested, her eyes looking over at Pam with a small smirk but Pam just gave a shake of her head.

"Good try but even I don't know exactly where Sanctuary is," Pam replied. "Although, I can promise you this trip won't be boring but not as dramatic as some you've taken."

"No ride or die through a cornfield?" Chance asked drolly. The ride through the cornfield in the mining cart to the Hunter's hideout still lingered with them, they had thought they were about to die when the cart careened at high speed to the blockade but instead they disappeared into the earth and down to Rouge Headquarters.

Pam laughed at his tone. "No and no flight in a glass bubble either."

"That one wasn't so bad," Chad interjected. They had to agree, when they visited the Sanctuary in Alaska they had enjoyed the flight in the glass bubble above Alaska. Even Cole who didn't like heights that much, although he tried to act tough about it.

Telara crossed her arms and leaned slightly back looking over the barrier in front of them. "So … how is this going to get us to Georgia?"

"Glad you asked." Pam gave a grin as she pulled her Crim from her belt with a flourish. Telara raised a brow but stayed silent as she waited, not something she was good at but she was learning. Turning around Pam placed the gem tip of her Crim against one of the many decorative wooden knots in the tree limbs that made up the wall before them. The gem started to glow and then the glow seeped into the wood as it expanded, one ringlet at a time until it consumed a good portion of the wall before them. With a satisfied look on her face, Pam put her Crim back on her leather belt around her waist as she turned back to them. "Last call for Georgia." Then laughed as she leapt through the glowing wall before them.

"A portal to Georgia here?" Chad's eyes were almost wider than the portal before them. "Static!" With that shout he took off running and cannonballed through the portal shouting, "Cowabunga!"

Tia looked over at Telara who just gave a shake of

her head, "I hope he didn't charge into Pam." Telara's eyes widened at Tia's remark, she hadn't thought about that.

"Oh, I hope he did!" Cole's eyes lit up. "I would *so* pay to see that!" He turned and ran quickly through the portal.

"With friends like him, who needs enemies?" Chance chuckled. "Better go make sure my brother is in one piece." He walked easily through the portal.

"One would think I would be used to events such as this happening regularly around me," I.Q. mused as he moved closer to the portal. Examining it as if he wished he could put it underneath a microscope and study it, which if it was possible, he probably would. Giving a lift of his shoulders, he moved through the portal and disappeared along with the rest of them.

Vanna looked over at Tia and Telara. "We aren't going to let the guys have all the fun are we?"

They both laughed and shook their heads. "No way!"

The three walked calmly through the portal together.

As soon as Telara entered the portal she felt as if something was off, no longer was she standing in between Tia and Vanna but was now by herself with lights zooming around her so fast they looked as if they were continuous. No more trees, no more ground, no more nothing. Looking around all she could see was light pink but when she reached out to touch, there was nothing. No way to tell which way to move, how to go back or go forward. She stumbled forward.

"Hey!" Tia laughed, grabbing her arm. "Chad missed Pam but you almost took her out."

Telara looked around in amazement, they were

standing outside a building in a parking lot. Gone was the pink atmosphere and zooming lights. Telara could feel the heat from the sun shining down on them and the hardness of the pavement beneath her feet. "That was weird."

"What?" Vanna turned to look at her.

"That pink air with zooming lights." Telara frowned at her. "I know we have seen some weird things but you guys have to admit even that was weirder than most."

"What pink air?" Tia turned.

"Zooming lights?" Cole looked around him for the lights.

Telara's brow furrowed. "Not funny guys!"

Pam looked at Telara, concern shining from her eyes. "Are you feeling okay? I haven't heard anyone having any reaction from the portals before, but there is always a first time."

Telara looked around her, feeling a tad sick to her stomach but she knew it wasn't a reaction to the portals but a reaction to this dawning realization. "You guys didn't see any pink or lights as you moved through the portal?"

Chance shook his head. "Didn't see anything, was in the forest then was here, like that," he gave a snap of his fingers as demonstration.

"I've never heard of anyone describing seeing anything as they moved through the portals," Pam mused.

Telara gave a silent groan, she hated being the one always dealing with any anomalies that pop up. "Forget it," she grumbled.

"Doesn't mean that no one has ever experienced it," Pam tried to reassure her. "Just that they never said anything."

"Then they were the smart ones." Telara had never wished she could take something back as bad as she did right now.

"Smart ones? You must be talking about me."

The cocky voice came from the shadows of the building they were in front of, the speaker moving with ease into the light, his grin matching his tone.

"Welcome to Georgia."

CHAPTER 4

L ogan." Pam said in greeting.

Standing there with one hand in his pocket while he raised the other in a sort of an offset salute was the one Pam had called Logan. He looked at them with a slanted grin and shaggy dark blond hair that fell over his eyes in curly locks. Sandals, cargo shorts, tank top with a multi-colored print buttoned up shirt completed his attire.

Can we say hang ten? Cole mentally quipped barely holding back his mirth.

Tia frowned at him. *Hang ten?*

His clothes! Chad tried to not be so obvious when he gave a shake of his head but from the narrowing of Pam's eyes, it wasn't working. Tia's glare wasn't helping their air of innocence either.

Surfer boy, Chance shot back as he watched Logan, nothing to show that he was having a mental conversation.

Pam turned back to Logan, who was still standing there with that slanted grin. "What's up with the destination?"

"Sorry about that." Logan gave a shrug of one of his muscular shoulders even though his expression showed no regret. "Transporter pad is being serviced, had to re-direct the portal outside the park gift shop."

Looking around they saw they were indeed in front of a building with a sign that said gift shop as well as other signs telling of the National Park they were standing in. "So, the Georgian Sanctuary is in a National Park?" Chad's voice rose in excitement. "Static!"

Logan looked their way, his slanted grin fading as he looked thoughtful. "We weren't told about any extra passengers."

"Wasn't planned, Logan," Pam told him.

"Ahhh." Logan gave a knowing nod.

Here it comes. Cole grinned. *Either Guardian envy or Guardian love.*

"Must be little siblings you had to bring with you so momma and daddy can have some alone time?" Logan's slanted grin was back.

Or neither. Tia could barely keep her snickering to herself.

"Siblings?" Chad's brows rose at him.

Logan lifted a placating hand. "No worries, little bro, Pam is family here so any of her family is welcome as well."

Vanna was joining Tia in stifling their snickers, barely.

"We're not siblings." I.Q. shook his head with a rueful look, keeping his gaze away from Chad and Cole who were both looking rather insulted.

"Stowaways?" Logan suggested with a twinkle in his eye. "Think we have someone here who knows how to play the flute, our own pied piper who can spin a tune you can dance to while the adults chat."

"Dude!" Cole practically spat out, his hands wide open at his sides as he stared at Logan. "We're the—"

Pam held up her hand, laughing,. "Relax Cole, he knows who you are, he is just yanking your chain. There isn't a Sanctuary outpost that doesn't know who you guys are."

Logan gave a crestfallen look. "Pammy! How could you? You took away my fun!" Pam just smirked. "When Reggie said you were coming, he never said anything about tagalongs. I could've been better prepared and had even more fun." His twinkle was practically dancing in his eyes at this point.

Every place has to have their comedian. Telara looked over at Cole and Chad who both gave her affronted looks.

"Wasn't planned," Pam told him. "Thought they might enjoy some of your guy's stories."

Yet another grin from Logan. "We have plenty of those."

"Exactly." Pam agreed. "So, where's Reggie? I expected to see him when I got here."

The slip in Logan's expression was only slightly noticeable, if not for all their training at Sanctuary they wouldn't have noticed it. His twinkle even dimmed a tad, their stomachs tightened as the air around them seemed to darken with the mood.

That's not a good sign. They could feel Vanna's apprehension.

"Reggie is at the square checking out the latest disappearances," a feminine voice that held an edge spoke from the shadows of the gift shop building. They watched as she moved from the shadows, her spiky green hair glinted in the sunlight and shades balancing on the bridge of her nose. Her sharp green eyes looked at them over the top of her shades as she joined Logan, barely coming to his shoulder and he wasn't that tall. His personality was taller, and the sass that seemed to drip from the newbie elevated her height better than her commando boots she was wearing. Green shorts, short shirt and band around her thigh.

Logan looked down at her. "You were supposed to wait at the camp."

"You were taking too long," she shot right back then looked over at the Guardians. "Who're the gatecrashers?"

"Really?" Cole exploded as everyone laughed, Chance had even fallen over in mirth.

"Meet Billie." Logan turned and started to walk towards the entrance to the gift shop cum welcome center. "I'm sure Zane will find somewhere to put the tag alongs while we take care of business, there's always the stables or even the Coliseum."

"We're right here!" Chad and Cole were glaring at Logan and while the rest of the Guardian's expressions were becoming unsettled, Vanna on the other hand was staring at Logan.

"Stables? As in horses?" The excitement in her voice also shined from her eyes at the thought of horses.

Billie did a half turn as she kept moving forward, not pausing a single stride. "Horses, unicorns, pegasi. What else do you think would be in a stable?" With that she turned back, moving past the cashier, who was handing change back to a tourist who was handing a stuffed cat to their child. The cashier barely looked their way. A soft meow had them looking down to see an orange tiger cat looking up at them.

"Ahhhhh," Vanna crooned as she leaned down to pet the cat, who was already weaving between her legs.

"Let's go Van," Chance called as they headed out the back glass door, all grinning as she reluctantly moved away from the cat that hobbled after her as she walked away. "Unicorns and pegasuses to play with but she can't leave a cat."

"Pegasi," I.Q. corrected.

Chance frowned at him. "Huh?"

"The plural of pegasus is pegasi," I.Q. told him as they moved into the warm Georgian sun behind the gift center. Chance rolled his eyes while the others' lips twitched in amusement.

"Are those spider webs hanging from the trees?"

"What?" Telara jerked at Cole's question looking up at the trees with wide eyes and gaped mouth.

"Spider webs?" Logan turned to look at Cole. "What spider webs?"

Billie started laughing. "I think he means the Spanish moss."

"That isn't moss, moss is green and grows on the trunks of trees not hanging down from trees," Chad protested looking up into the trees at the gray strands hanging down.

Billie looked over at Chad and shook her head with an eye roll. "Whatever, man. You know best."

Tia reached up and pulled some down from a nearby tree that was hanging down low. "It's awful soft." She rubbed it against her cheek looking at Telara. "We could take some of this home and make some awesome pillow stuffing out of it."

Logan looked at her, the corners of his mouth

twitching so much it looked like he was having a seizure or something. "Sure ya can, if you don't mind the bugs."

Tia's eyes went wide before she threw the Spanish moss on the ground and started swatting at her face to knock off the imaginary bugs, much to the mirth of everyone around her. Especially Chad and Cole who have been at the receiving end of most of Tia's little barbed remarks.

"Wasn't there a car maker who used the moss for seat stuffing and ended up having to recall all the vehicles when bugs came out of the seams?" Chad frowned looking up at the tree.

"That sounds like a horror movie." Tia looked up at that tree with a disgusted look.

"Let's go." Pam tried to hide her smile as they followed her past a big white house and several looking little sheds all in a line. Tia followed absently wiping at her face and running her fingers through her hair looking at the strands suspiciously.

Cole pointed to the wooden stakes that were half buried into the dirt at an angle as they walked over a wooden bridge. "Van Helsing's work?"

Billie looked back at him briefly before turning back and moving down the slanted hillside towards an opening in a nearby hill, the opening had a simple wooden frame around it. Looking around they saw several other open doorways in the hills.

"Tough audience," Cole grumbled as they moved through the doorway into the underground bunker.

"This is so cool," Chance breathed as he looked into the few rooms they passed. One showed a single bed with an old stove in the corner as well as a single table and chair.

"Commander's quarters," Pam supplied as they continued down the corridor into the back of the tunnel that opened up into the soldiers' quarters. Wooden bunk beds lined the wall to both sides with a very old looking fireplace in the back of the room.

Billie and Logan walked straight for the fireplace and looked back at them. "You coming or playing tourist?"

Tia frowned at Logan. "We get that you probably see all this everyday but this is new to us, we've never been here before and this is history." She gestured around the room.

"Not our history." Billie shrugged.

"What do you mean?" I.Q. tilted his head at her.

"This is Georgian history, not Arion history," Logan spoke up. "Our history is much different; we didn't participate in the wars of the past. Our wars were fought against a true villain rather than each other. Now, if you guys are ready to see our home, follow us." A wink and he stepped through the fireplace and was gone.

Bille grinned and gave a jaunty wave before flipping right through the wall.

They looked at Pam, who just laughed. "You guys are seriously surprised?"

"Yeah, but we probably shouldn't be," Telara admitted wryly.

More laughter as Pam waved them forward. "Let's go, we have some answers to find." Only minimal pausing before they each moved through the fireplace portal.

Telara opened her eyes to the brightness around her and the bustle of activity, thankful there was no pink air or fluttering lights. Logan and Billie were speaking to two guys who were pointing away from them as they spoke animatedly. Looking around Telara saw more wooden frames in hills that were larger than those in the state park they just came from. To the left there were four frames in different hills, different sizes and different symbols etched along the frame. Each frame had doors that were closed and no door was the same.

The first one seemed rather plain with a curved lever handle that was dark bronze in color, the design on the door looked as if there was a flower in the middle of several circles with different scenes within. Telara squinted to try to see some of the scenes when a shadow fell over them, they turned to see a guy looking at them, his lips beneath his blond mustache pulled into a half grin as they realized he had been watching them gawking for more than a moment.

"Hi." Telara awkwardly waved at the man who was looking at them. He had a relaxed demeanor as he stood there in jeans with leather boots and buttoned shirt that was rolled up to his elbows. His blond hair was curling around his ears and just past his neck with darkened blond curls. Sharp blue eyes seemed to catch every detail as his gaze had looked over them all before coming back to rest on Telara making her fidget, feeling as if she was being examined to the bone.

"Zane." Logan broke away from Billie and the two still animated guys who were still gesturing around them.

"Logan," Zane acknowledged him without looking away from Telara. "Were we expecting extra guests?"

Cole and Chad both sighed. *Here we go again.*

Vanna elbowed the one closest to her, which happened to be Chad, "ouch!" Logan snickered but Zane was still watching Telara. She tried to not notice that fact but she was finding it tough.

"It was a last-minute decision," Pam told him, moving forward.

Cole burst out, "And we aren't stowaways, extras or add ons. We're the Guardians!"

Telara did half an eye roll while shaking her head giving a halfhearted, embarrassed chuckle.

Zane's laughter barked out, "the Guardians are always welcome here."

Billie snorted, ignoring the perplexed looks that were sent her way. "Didn't think they were allowed here," she grumbled sotto voce.

Zane gave a shrug of his muscular shoulder under his shirt. "Guess Lucius had a change of heart." His manner showed he could care less but Telara felt as if there was something beneath the surface that belied his uncaring manner.

"Actually Lucius didn't want us to come," she admitted, watching Zane's eyes darken at her words, another clue that he cared more than he was letting on. "We decided it wasn't his decision." She hated seeing his eyes darken, she wasn't sure why but she really did. So, when he grinned at her last statement, she felt really good and returned his grin. She didn't even acknowledge Billie's snort before she stalked off. Whatever problem Billie had with them was Billie's problem, not anyone else's.

"A rebel." Zane gave an approving smile. "I like it. How about I show you guys around our humble home?"

"I like that idea," Telara responded as they followed Zane.

CHAPTER 5

They moved closer to the four doors in the hillside with the etchings, listening as Zane told them about Haven, how they had even been there during the battles that took place at Fort McAllister. "There were several battles before Major General William T. Sherman finally captured Savanna the Christmas of 1864."

"You had the same entrance to Haven back then?" I.Q. asked, when Zane nodded, he continued. "You never once got caught by any of the troops that were fighting?"

Zane chuckled, "I never said that."

"Really?" Now he had Chad and Cole's attention. "What happened?" they both asked.

"Made a few of the troops go sober, well, for a few days," Zane told them. "Created some stories that were explained away as liquor induced." They laughed thinking about what type of stories could've been told, stopping when Zane turned to them. "These here are the lodgings for Haven as well as guest quarters." He motioned towards the doors that Telara had been looking at before. She could now see the scenes within the circles and some of them reminded her of the scenes they saw in

Soleil's bubbles back in Alaska. The other doors had decorative etchings and wooden sculptures built into them of different types of animals, one looked like a hawk while another resembled a wolf. Not one was the same.

They walked past the four doors in the hills, curious if they were just like the ones they had left with the rows of wooden bunk beds or if they were something more magical like back at Sanctuary or the Hunter's Citadel.

They aren't small like those we just left, Vanna spoke mentally as she looked over at the hills.

You can tell how big they are? I.Q. looked at her in surprise. *Can you tell if they are rustic or full of magic?*

She shook her head. *I just know their size is vast.*

"Am I boring you?" Zane looked at them curiously but Pam gave them a look that told them she knew what they were doing and wasn't amused.

"Sorry." Vanna looked abashed but Zane just laughed.

"No worries, I understand enjoying having your own private conversation but make sure you don't miss out what is happening around you." They stared dumbfounded at Zane, Pam hadn't even realized what they were doing until they explained it to her. Wide eyed they looked at each other.

Think we should be careful.

Tia nodded at Telara's words before turning back to Zane as he pointed to another door in a hill that was situated away from everything else. "That is our gym and training center, if you feel like working out while you are here, feel free." Turning around he pointed to the structure that dominated the center of the Haven, tall white columns that resembled those from ancient Greece. "That is our Coliseum where we like to have nightly shows."

"Nightly shows?" Chad stared at the Coliseum with a longing expression.

"A good way to unwind," Zane turned and pointed to another doorway in a hill but they could also see doorways along the side with double doors on top and bottom. "There you will find our stables."

"Do you really have unicorns and pegasi?" Vanna stared at the stables with the same longing as Chad had stared at the Coliseum.

Zane chuckled. "We do, I'll have Billie introduce you to them later."

"Really?"

The rest of them laughed at the look on Vanna's face, Zane had just made some extra points with their Mother Nature.

"Of course." He agreed as he pointed to the lake next to the stables, where trees created nice shady areas around the lake. "We also have a swimming hole, which, just like everything here, you're welcome to enjoy." He turned to the right pointing off to his left where they can see a larger size hill with two double doors that looked as if a whole convoy of trucks could drive through. "Our headquarters are through those doors, not as big as Sanctuary nor do we have all the neat toys they do but it fits us just fine." He gave a half-hearted shrug then gave a sly look, "we still manage to take care of our own and even have toys of our own."

Tia looked sideways at him. "Really?"

Zane gave a nod as he kept walking to the other side of the Coliseum to where three decent sized hills could be seen with wooden doors that had different etchings of their own. "Cafeteria and our own recreation areas are in the first building with the community center next and the one that is further back and not as large is the crystal warehouse."

"You mean the ones they allow us." Logan's sardonic voice surprised them as he had come up from behind them.

"Don't you guys have your own Crims?" Telara asked and then looked at Pam who had been unusually silent during the tour. Most noticeably during the snarky remarks about what Sanctuary allowed them.

Billie pulled out a pen that was on a silver chain and twirled it around her finger. "Oh, we get them. We have to make sure to account for every single one and even have a representative that likes to visit to make sure we don't have any extras."

They looked at each other but weren't really sure how to react to her statements, something just didn't feel exactly right. Pam's silence made it even more awkward.

"We make do, Billie." Zane's soft words reminded Telara of Lucius.

Billie smiled brightly at him. "Yes we do." Turning to them she pointed to the flat area past the crystal warehouse. "There are our training areas, hand to hand." They could see several Arions there now grappling with each other while a trainer watched them. "Weapons," Arions were fighting with staffs, swords, batons and other weapons on the other side of the wrestling Arions. "There is also a track and our own little obstacle course."

"Does it have its own lava pit?" Cole quipped.

"You're welcome to find out." Billie smirked at him.

"Yeah, not trusting that smile." Cole shook his head and everyone laughed.

"Good plan." Logan smirked, then looked over at Pam. "You're welcome to grab a bite to eat before Reggie gets back." Cole's stomach started grumbling, and then Chad's let out a loud growl causing everyone to laugh. "That sounds like a unanimous decision."

Zane placed his hand on Logan's shoulder. "Show our guests to the cafeteria and make sure they are taken care of while I get some work done, that way when Reggie gets back, he won't be bogged down with paperwork." He grinned at the Guardians. "I look forward to meeting with all of you later." He looked at Telara with a strange brightness in his eyes before turning around quickly and striding away towards the barracks.

"Let's go ladies and gents." Logan winked at them, turning around, moving away from them without another word, leaving them to scurry to catch up to him.

"Going to tell me about the disappearances Billie spoke of?" Logan was just taking a big bite of his meatball sub when Pam asked.

After swallowing the bite, he leaned over and wiped his pizza sauce-covered mouth on Vanna's white tee before turning around to face Pam who was sitting next to him.

"Hey!" Van looked down at the offending bright red stain then glared at Logan whose back was to her. If Logan had paid attention to the Guardians sitting at the table, he would've saw that they put their food and utensils down looking very warily towards Vanna. That might have been a warning for him, possibly. But he hadn't and when one of the potted green plants in the cafeteria started to move one of its green stems along the floor, growing in size the closer it got to the table, the Guardians looked down watching it weave between their feet towards their goal.

If Logan had been paying attention he might have noticed the Guardians moving so that they were further from him, instead he kept talking to Pam, "No one is allowed out on patrol alone anymore, we're even encouraged to – HEY!"

Pam's eyes grew wide as she watched the green stem that resembled a giant Python wrap around Logan's waist and chest, lifting him up from the bench he was sitting on at the lunch table.

"What is this?" Logan looked around as he struggled to release himself from the snake-like plant that had him in its clutches.

Vanna rose, then reached over to grab Logan's bottle of water, wetting down the napkins that Tia and I.Q. had passed her way. Then she proceeded to dab at her shirt doing her best to get out the stain, her brows furrowed in concentration.

"Hey!" Logan shouted at her as the plant twirled him around so that he was now hanging upside down. "Let me down!"

Vanna looked around the room, looking perplexed. Billie, who was sitting on the other side of the table at the end, ate her salad, not even paying any attention to Logan or Vanna. Vanna looked at her. "Do you have any lemon juice?" she asked, the tone of her voice showing none of the anger from earlier. Billie looked up, then gestured towards a silver fridge with glass doors next to the condiment table. "Thank you." Vanna looked back at the potted plant who was already moving another green stem to the fridge, opening it up and grabbing the lemon juice. When the stem reached Vanna, she took the bottle with a smile. She soaked some more napkins in lemon juice and continued dabbing at the stain.

"All right!" Logan shouted. "I'm sorry, okay?"

Vanna glared at the stain that wasn't as dark but clearly still there then looked up at Logan with a dark look. It seemed Logan finally realized the situation he was in; his face lost the bronze tan and became pasty white.

"I'll get you a new shirt," he offered but when she simply raised a brow he continued, "and I won't do it again, I promise!"

Vanna gave a half snort, half sigh before flicking her wrist. Logan ended up on the floor on his back as the stem shrunk in size and moved back to the dirt in the pot. "You will get me a new shirt, not white, and learn manners." With those words, she sat down to finish her salad still looking disgruntled. "Wonder if I could talk Lucius into getting me some of that fabric they use on the furniture back in Sanctuary," she grumbled darkly while Logan was dusting himself off watching her closely as he attempted to sit back down.

"You were encouraged to…" Pam prompted him as she took a drink of her pop.

Logan turned and stared at her before looking back at Vanna and then Pam with an incredulous look but she just looked at him, waiting for him to answer. It took him a few more moments and one last nervous look towards Vanna before he finally spoke again, "we were encouraged to go out in groups, at least three or more."

"Shadow attacks?" Pam asked, popping a chip in her mouth.

Logan gave a slight lift of his shoulder, quickly looking at Vanna before turning slowly back to Pam who was having a hard time hiding her amusement at his expense. "No clue, these are stealth disappearances that happen when no one is suspecting with no evidence. No Shadow attacks, a few have been during patrol but there were some that happened during some downtime. Leslie went out to go shopping and never returned, hell, Jack went to bed one night and when we went to his room it was empty the next morning."

"When did this start?" When he didn't answer her, Pam suggested sweetly, "I could always have Vanna ask."

Logan blanched at her words, looking over at Vanna, who didn't seem to even be paying attention to the conversation, but by the twinkle in her eye, Telara and the other Guardians knew she was listening to every word. Logan scooted closer to Pam and away from Vanna before responding, "Before summer."

"What?" Pam stared at him. "Why didn't you say something sooner? Why not when you requested me to come here? We need the Alpha faction here and maybe some of the others."

Logan shook his head. "Nope, Zane said only you and that took some fancy talking. You know he isn't one to trust easily. Trusts only family, and if you weren't grandfathered in, I doubt he would've allowed us to call you."

"Lucky me," Pam said wryly.

"He knows Ira would do anything to replace him," Logan spoke matter-of-factly.

"He really should speak to Lucius." Pam turned her body completely to face him. "He might be able to help him."

Logan gave a shake of his head, his shaggy hair flying with the motion. "Nope, he won't even talk to your Caretaker." He snorted. "Barely says his name. Wish I knew what he had against him." The last sentence was spoken softly as if he was speaking to himself.

"He doesn't like Lucius?"

"Ewww." Tia sent a gust of wind at Cole to close his mouth that was full of food. "Swallow before you speak." She wrinkled her nose in distaste at him, she always hated when he did that.

Cole swallowed before asking Logan, "Why?"

"You go ahead and ask him yourself," Logan suggested as he rose. "See if he will tell you." He grabbed his empty dishes moving to the garbage, throwing out the throwaways and putting the dishes in the bin on top. Turning to look at them he asked. "How about you come see tonight's show at the Coliseum? Reggie is supposed to be there as well."

CHAPTER 6

The seats of the Coliseum were nothing more than stone benches that curved around the center of the Coliseum where a stage that any Broadway actor or actress would be jealous of. The size rivaled any they had ever seen, in person or on the tube. There weren't any cloth backdrops with images that needed to be changed, the background changed so seamlessly that they were sure there were illusion crystals doing the work. Although the props on the stage had them stumped, changing so seamlessly, but they were more than illusions. Solid enough for one of the performers to be able to touch, move or even sit on.

Telara looked over at I.Q. who was staring very intently at the stage, another enigma that had no explanation. Whenever they thought they had the handle on this new world they lived in, something would happen that would send them spinning yet again.

Pulling up her legs and tucking them underneath her on the hard bench, she turned her attention back to the story playing out in front of them on the stage. It wasn't any story that she had ever heard of, she wondered if they created their own plays here.

If so, this person should take these to Hollywood. This would make an awesome movie. Chad was glued to the play and the others gave very mild nods in agreement with his remark.

The world that came alive on the stage in front of them was a world that none of them had ever seen. No Crims, no crystals and no fun. This world was ruled by one that was referred to as the Supreme Ruler, who struck fear into all with their army. They watched as the people of this world lived in poverty, some stealing just to survive but all living in fear. Any small infraction was dealt with dire consequences, getting caught stealing a piece of bread would impose a twenty-year imprisonment.

Yikes! Chad and Cole looked at each other. *I don't think we could survive in that land.*

The stage cleared and now they saw someone in a cloak moving through the streets of the town, throwing out furtive glances around her. She entered one of the buildings and the stage turned so that they could see inside the building where others were moving to quickly pull down the cloth curtains, dashing out the candles and shutting the wooden doors. When they were done, they gathered around the table.

"Another one has gone missing," the cloaked female spoke as she removed the hood, revealing her pulled back blond hair and porcelain white features.

"Do we know for sure if she is the one who is taking them?" a hulking figure that hunkered down in the corner asked, his voice gruff and coarse.

"Who else is there?" another feminine voice spoke up as she moved from the shadows although her features were hidden beneath a cloak of her own. It seemed that even hidden in this place from outside eyes, they were still keeping their identities hidden except for the one who must be their leader, the blond standing there.

"Do we even know what she's looking for?" another male spoke from the shadows.

This time it was the blond-haired leader who spoke, "Not yet, but we will."

The stage went dark as the scenery changed once again, this time they saw the blond-haired leader attempting to break into a very guarded building only to get captured by several soldiers in dark uniforms and metal helmets that hid their identity completely. Her trial was like nothing they had ever seen, there were three very elderly men whose faces looked like they were permanently sour looking sitting behind a tall desk with three very high-backed black chairs. There were no charges announced, no chance for the defense to speak, nothing that resembled a true court. The three men sentenced the woman to life in prison.

They were silent as they watched the stage change yet again, they were waiting for the happy ending. After all, every story had a happy ending. They were practically sitting at the edge of their seats as they watched the next scene come to life. The stage lit up and the leader was huddled in a corner in a dark cell, the floor was dirty with pieces of straw and dust covering it. As they watched, the wall behind the woman opened and a robust figure moved into the cell. The woman rolled out of his way and held up a bucket that was on the floor in front of her as if to use it as a weapon.

"You would try to attack your savior?" They heard the amused masculine voice ask her, pausing her movement of swinging the bucket at him.

"Savior?" She frowned at him.

"Well, attempting savior," he told her then looking towards the door of the cell, they both heard voices. "We need to go ... NOW!" He kept his voice low but firm as he beckoned her to go with him. She gave him a tentative smile, the door a nervous glance then put her hand in his.

The lights dimmed and the stage went dark, then all lights were shining brightly and there on the stage were the actors taking a bow.

Why does every story have to have a sappy element to it?

Shut it! Tia glared at Cole, who snorted.

Guys... Vanna spoke through their mental link warningly, staring straight at the stage. Telara glanced over to where Pam, Logan and Billie were sitting. Zane was watching them with a grin, there were two guys standing next to him that they hadn't seen before. Of course, there were many here they hadn't met yet. One watched them with dark eyes from beneath his dark braids that hung down, the other had a spiky green mohawk and arms crossed over his bulky chest. The one with dark braids wore an orange and black tank top with tattered jeans and dusty looking sandals.

Mohawk dude just needs a feathered headset and leather breeches with fringes.

Cole looked over at Chad with wide eyes, *Dude, you're going to end up dead.*

What? Chad looked confused.

Guys... Vanna growled at them, finally they took the hint. They turned back to watch where the actors were still bowing trying to look as innocent as they could, which probably wasn't fooling anyone. Standing up they clapped with the others, Cole and Chad went even as far as to start shouting out their enjoyment while they stood on the stone benches. Telara and Tia looked at each other laughing, they had to agree that it was very entertaining. Moving over to where Pam stood with Logan, Billie and now Zane with his two comrades, they smiled as Zane introduced them to the two newcomers.

"Reggie, Billy, meet the Guardians." Zane gestured to each of them as he introduced them by name.

"Billy?" Chad looked from Billy with his green mohawk and husky physique standing there in his jeans, combat boots, white tank and tattered jean jacket to Billie with her green spiky hair who was watching him with a narrowed look, practically daring him to say what was on his mind. Telara sighed inwardly, something echoed by the others: never dare Chad or Cole, especially since both were good for not thinking before they speak.

"He's my twin brother," Billie told him dryly, no softening in her face as she watched him.

Oh no. Telara's dismay was written all over her face. Even though Pam couldn't hear her inward thoughts, she could see them all over face. Telara wasn't even hiding what she was thinking, neither were the others who wished that Chad had a better filter.

"Twins with the same name?"

Shut it, bro. Chance attempted to silence his brother when Billy crossed his arms over his chest looking at Chad. *That man looks like he could bench press three of you.*

"Don't tell me," Chad didn't stop as he looked at Billy and said, "Billy with an i-e." He said with flourish then turned to Billie and said with that same smirk, "and you are Billie with a y?"

Billy moved with a quickness no one expected; he went from standing next to Zane to right in front of Chad, staring right down at him. The fact that Chad was six foot tall and still had to tip his head back to look into Billy's face finally registered with him.

Ummmm, Cole?

Cole snorted moving back from his best bud, speaking out loud, "You're on your own, dude. Need to keep my handsome features free of scars for ladies, can't be upsetting them because you opened your mouth without thinking."

The whole Coliseum had gone quiet during this exchange, as everyone waited to see if Billy was going to send Chad sailing over the benches. The other Guardians stood there tense as they watched, they knew it was Chad's own fault but they didn't want him hurt because he didn't know how to keep his big mouth shut.

Thanks, Chad's wry voice told them he heard their thoughts as he swallowed hard still staring up at the giant that was Billy.

I tried to help, his brother shot back. *You ignored me so this one is all you, bro.*

"Any chance you're related to Claw?" Vanna asked Billy as she watched him closely.

Billy turned to look at her, his expression went from dark to curious. "Aren't you the one who put Logan on his head?"

The groan that accompanied that question was loud and in stereo, this situation just went from bad to worse.

Vanna nodded, which put them on high alert as they waited for Billy's response. They didn't have to wait long. A grin broke out on his face and he gently clapped her on the shoulder. "About time someone put that loud mouth in his place," they breathed a very audible sigh of relief. Billy tilted his head towards Chad. "You should try that on this one."

Vanna grimaced. "I've tried. Too much of a hard head."

Billy let out a bark of laughter turning around walking over to where his sister stood watching the exchange. His sister looked over at Vanna, looking impressed. "My brother doesn't take a liking to too many."

Billy snorted. "Who said I took a liking to her?"

"Just like you didn't take a liking to Lucy." Reggie ribbed him.

Billy's broad shoulders lifted in a nonchalant manner. "I didn't, she's my servant, so I have to put up with her."

They watched his sister roll her eyes while Reggie half grunted, half laughed. Vanna frowned at him. "Servant?"

"Wait." Cole frowned, looking at each of them standing there. "Lucy from the Citadel?"

Billie nodded. "The same."

Telara's brow crinkled. "She lets you call her your servant?"

"She doesn't have a choice." Billy didn't seem to notice their perplexed looks, either that or he didn't care.

His sister moved forward shaking her head. "It's an ongoing battle between the two, she gives as good as she gets." Billy snorted at her but she just waved it off. "I don't even ask anymore."

"Nothing to ask about," her brother retorted, "that's just the way it is."

"Says who?" Vanna frowned at him.

"Me." Billy stared at Vanna, her darkening looks didn't seem to faze him one bit. He didn't look away until his sister patted his chest."

"Sure it is, bro," She smirked at her brother walking away while Zane laughed. Her brother moved swifter than anyone thought was possible, he wasn't small by any means, picking up his sister he tossed her over his shoulder and headed towards the lake.

"Sounds like you need a Lucy-like dip in the Lake." Billy strode away with his sister hitting his back.

Zane watched them leave with amusement, "seems we're getting unending entertainment tonight."

Chad chuckled. "Those two do seem amusing."

Reggie let out a rough laugh. "The boss man was speaking about you, man."

"Hey!" Chad protested; laughter filled the night air.

Zane waved at them to follow him. "Let's get you guys settled for the night, tomorrow you guys will see another show. Hopefully, one on the stage." His amusement was clear in his voice as he moved towards the barracks he had shown them earlier.

Following him they looked over towards the lake expecting to see the Billies there but they couldn't see anything between the trees. With the moon shining down the whole area was illuminated, but the brother and sister were nowhere to be seen.

Thought he said he was throwing her in the water, Cole mused as they walked.

Vanna shrugged. *Maybe he realized how unreasonable he was being.*

Highly doubt that. Telara did her best to keep her mirth from her expression but one glance at Zane who was grinning even as he said nothing, had her feeling that he knew they were chatting via their personal link. *Billy doesn't seem like the type to admit he could be in the wrong.*

CHAPTER 7

Telara looked around the sitting room situated outside their bedrooms, where they were sitting with Pam, none ready to go to bed just yet. There was no sci-fi feel about the room like the Command Center nor the fantasy feel of their bungalow here. The walls were dirt as well as the floor but the floor felt as solid as a concrete one. The chairs and sofas were nothing special, comfortable to sit in but nothing like the white ones that soaked up all stains at the bungalow or sci-fi glass and shiny metal like at the Command Center back at Sanctuary.

"Feeling disappointed?" Pam asked them, her expression amused.

Telara didn't realize that their thoughts were written all over their faces, she felt her face grow warm. "Sorry, we didn't mean—

Pam laughed, shaking her head. "Don't worry about it, after all that you have seen this must be a bit … normal."

"That's one word for it," Cole said.

"I don't know that I would call this place normal." Vanna pulled her legs underneath her on the sofa she was sitting on. "Never saw any place with their own Coliseum with props and scenery like that."

"Or stories," Chad gushed. "That was a cool play we saw tonight; I want to see more."

"Me too." Chance nodded in agreement with his brother. "I want to see what happens next."

"Well, I don't have any plans to leave until I know what is going on with these disappearances." Pam dipped her head. "Something is going on and I want to know what it is."

"And we need to find out about that picture of Telara's clone," I.Q. reminded them.

Telara looked over at Pam. "Who do you think would be the best one for us to start asking about that?"

Pam chewed on her bottom lip, looking deep in thought for a few moments before responding, "Maybe find out who writes the plays, the one we saw tonight seemed vaguely familiar."

"What do you mean?" Tia cocked her head.

"I don't know really." Pam's expression was still thoughtful. "Something that I can't put my finger on but familiar."

"How do we find out who writes the plays?" Telara asked her, trying to stifle the yawn that wouldn't stay hidden.

Pam laughed as she stood up. "Stay here tomorrow while I go out on patrol with Reggie to see what is going on, keep your eyes and ears open. I'm sure you'll have many around here excited to be able to show the Guardians what they know."

Cole's eyes brightened. "You mean there are some who actually like the Guardians?"

"Logan and the Billies tend to give everyone a hard time, regardless of their status," Pam said, then yawned herself. "Let's see what we can find out tomorrow night, for now let's get some sleep." She walked towards the exit.

"Aren't you staying here with us?" Telara, who had stood up and moved towards the room they were told was for the girls, asked her.

Pam looked back at her. "As Alpha leader I have my own quarters here, but I'll see you tomorrow." With a wave, she was gone.

Telara looked over at the others who were heading to their respective doors and beds. With a sigh and shrug she followed Tia and Vanna, she was truly tired and looking forward to some sleep.

At first it was the sound of clinking glass that Telara heard, too tired to open her eyes just yet until a soft feminine humming reached her ears. Her eyes shot open as she stared up at what should have been the dirt ceiling. Instead, there was a soft pink canopy over her head. For a moment she couldn't move, her body felt frozen beneath the soft pink comforter that wasn't there when she went to sleep. Usually when she dreams with Zach, she wakes up in the same room she had fallen asleep in, this wasn't the same room.

Looking around her to see where she was, the first thing she noticed was the soft pink curtains that matched the fabric canopy overhead, surrounding the bed she was in. Reaching out, she pulled back the soft curtains to get out of the bed and ended up with a face full of sheer, lightweight Chiffon that felt scratchy against her cheek. With a grunt she pushed it aside as well standing up on the cold hard floor. Looking down at her bare feet she saw a white and pink tiled floor instead of dirt.

"Nope, not in Kansas anymore," she muttered to herself. Her eyes lit up when she saw the pink slippers right there on the floor, as if waiting for her. Of course, they could be. Crazier things have happened. Now that her feet were encased in the warm slippers she needed to figure out where she was and see if she was dreaming or not.

Dreaming! She looked around for Zach, dreams meant Zach and maybe he might have some answers for her. Her brow furrowed as she looked around the room. "Zach?"

Moving around the room she saw a crystal bowl situated on top of a six-drawer dresser with intricate swirls and lines carved in the front of each drawer. The foot of each leg curled up in a swirl that looked as if it curled right back into the leg and crawled right back up the dresser. Moving to the dresser she noticed several other crystal pieces laying across the top, situated around the bowl.

She picked up a crystal pointed tower, rolling it between her fingers, then placed it next to what looked like a crystal pendulum minus the chain. Her fingers touched the tips of a crystal cluster, which resembled a mini version of a parent crystal. On the other side of the bowl were two more clusters, one just a bit thicker than the other. They weren't like any Crims she knew of or any of the crystals back at Sanctuary.

Well, except for the mini crystal clusters, she thought to herself.

The humming started back up again, pulling her attention from the crystals. Looking around the room she felt as if she was starring in a fairy tale story. The walls resembled the tree bark walls back at Vanna's room in the Bungalow back at Sanctuary. There was an arched wooden door on the other side of the room but the humming was coming from behind her, where there was an opening in the wall with a cloth curtain hanging there.

Pushing aside the curtain, she peered through the opening into a room that looked as if it was part of the same fairy tale story, except this one was the one where the witch did her magic with all her potions. The room looked as if it was built into a tree with wooden cupboards along the walls, shelves on one side of the room and over the table that looked as if it was hundreds of years old.

A bright light she saw out of the corner of her eye captured her attention, she turned but all she could see was a pale slender hand reaching for one of the many colorful glass jars on the shelves. On the wrist was a silver bracelet with gems, ornate charms and a small glass vial with a wooden cork dangling down catching the light from the window from high. The light from the window shined down brightly, making it so she couldn't see the person who was humming as she poured out some crystal pieces onto a colorful glass tray.

This wasn't Zach, that she was sure of but she wanted to know who had brought her to this place and why. She pushed the curtain further open, attempting to move further into the room so that she could see the humming witch. She had some questions that needed answers.

"Telly!"

She jerked and there was Tia staring down at her.

Gone was the fairy tale room, humming witch and any answers she wanted to get.

"Morning sleepyhead!"

Telara groaned and rubbed her face with a groan. "Why is it my dreams that get hijacked?"

Tia plopped down on her bed with Vanna following by leaping on the bed. "Hey!" If not for Tia's quick gust of wind, Telara would have landed on the floor with a crash, instead she was lifted up before she hit the floor and settled back up on the bed to look at the two sets of very wide eyes staring at her.

"Zach?" they asked in unison, both leaning on their elbows with bright eyes.

Telara sighed. "I wish."

The expressions went from curious to confused. "Thought you said your dream was hijacked? Who else hijacks your dreams?"

"Did we hear something about Zach?" Standing there in the doorway were the guys with the same curious looks they shared when it came to Zach. Telara had the same curiosity even though she was the one who got to talk to him.

"It wasn't Zach." The dejected tone of Telara's voice matched the disappointed looks on her friends. "I have no idea who it was, I wish I did."

"What did the person look like?" Tia asked her.

"A very pale hand with skinny fingers and a silver bracelet that had crystal charms on it," Telara said with a grimace. "That was all I saw."

"So, a female version of Thing?" Chad asked.

"You were dream-napped by the Addams Family?" Vanna perked up from her position on the bed.

"Hate to break it to you guys but it definitely wasn't their house I woke up in, unless Wednesday's new favorite color is pink." Telara lifted a shoulder.

"No spider webs and creaky floor boards?" Chance laughed then ducked behind his brother when Telara leveled a narrowed look at him.

"No-o-o," she said slowly. "This place was more like out of a fairy tale, pink gossamer bedding on a canopy bed and a secret room that looked as if it was built within a tree. A secret room with shelves around the room that held glass bottles situated over a wooden table full of different types of instruments and more containers full of different stuff."

"Did this person say anything to you?" I.Q. asked her, watching her closely.

Telara shook her head, "nope, just hummed but then again, I don't think she saw me."

"You're sure it was a she?" Chance asked, trying to not look too skeptical, not that she could blame any of them. They only ever had her word to go on and they always took her at her word, none of them ever saw what she saw.

"I'm not sure of anything." Telara leaned back against the headboard with a disgruntled look. "I can only say what I saw but that doesn't help when I can't see everything, and when I do see someone I can talk to, they don't tell me everything but stupid riddles." Her voice rose in agitation as she spoke, the others could feel her frustration.

"Hey." Tia, the voice of reason, rolled off the bed. "Let's go grab some breakfast and see what the day holds for us."

"I wanna see if they have a sign-up sheet for the plays." Chad rubbed his hands together with bright eyes.

"What makes you think they would consider you?" His brother looked over at him, his lip curling.

Chad scoffed. "Everyone wants a piece of this." He pointed both thumbs at himself while the others laughed, moving out of the room to get ready for breakfast. "You all will see."

Tia and Vanna laughed while Telara just shook her head as they shut the door behind the boys. "Maybe some food will help," Telara conceded.

CHAPTER 8

Pam wasn't at breakfast when they got down to the cafeteria, Billy and his sister were just leaving. "Hey B1 and B2," Chad quipped with a grin that faltered as Billy glowered down at him.

"Let's go before you end up stuffed in a trash can," Vanna muttered, pushing Chad into the room and past the brother and sister.

The rest moved quickly past the glowering duo shooting them nervous glances.

"Are you insane?" Vanna asked him, shoving him forward towards the breakfast buffet. "Want to go home and call Claw porcupine head next?"

That brought a few flinches from the others as well as groans.

"Food, then we find Pam," Telara said, shaking her head as she grabbed her food, moving to a nearby table to eat. The others nodded, grabbing their food as well.

They found Pam by the training grounds with Reggie and two others who were putting on thick black plastic looking bracelets on their wrists. The expressions on the two guys that Pam and Reggie were talking to became guarded when Telara and the others reached them. The shorter one was wearing a ball cap, his thin hair sticking out from underneath it as if he was related to Fritz. His clothes were nothing special—t-shirt, jeans and running shoes. His companion was dressed in camouflage pants, boots, green tank top with a too heavy for the Georgian sun green long jacket. Dark, greasy hair, bushy brows with eyes that looked to be in a permanent squint.

Neither seemed thrilled to see them.

"Hey." Telara looked away from them to Pam as they reached her.

Reggie gave a wave as he and the other two moved away. "We'll wait for ya at the entrance." He took off without waiting for Pam to respond.

"What are those?" Tia pointed towards the bracelet on Pam's wrist that matched the same ones they saw Reggie and the other two putting on their wrists.

"New suits Claw has been working on, he had them sent over this morning," Pam told them, moving her arm so that the sleeve of her light jacket covered the bracelet.

"What does it do?" Telara tilted her head.

"Creates a full body suit that makes it so you can blend completely into whatever background you're standing in front of." Pam explained. "He's been waiting for someone to be able to test them out in the field."

"Static!" Chad's eyes brightened. "Where's ours?"

"You guys are staying here," Pam informed him, she put both hands up as they frowned at her. "Hear me out." She waited for them to settle back silently. "You need to find out about the past Guardians and you have to stay here to do that."

"So what? We've been demoted to research?" Telara

crossed her arms, not sure why it was bothering her so much that Pam was going out without them. All she did know was that something was feeling off about all this.

Pam turned to look at her. "If research saves your lives, then yes, research. Remember the reason that we came here?"

Telara bit her lip looking down wishing she could take back her ill-thought question.

Pam sighed. "They're already suspicious about why you guys are here, I told them you liked the idea of learning more about the stories they tell of the Guardians to help you with your re—" She stopped and corrected herself. "Sleuthing. We don't want them getting suspicious."

Telara grimaced, hating that Pam felt she had to censor what she said so as not to upset her.

"I get the feeling that some here aren't too happy to see us," Tia spoke up.

Pam gave a halfhearted snort. "They don't trust too many here."

"Why?" Telara's curiosity rode over her earlier chagrin.

Pam looked back to the hillside opening where Reggie and the other two had disappeared through. "It's a long story but mainly has to do with the fact that Ira and even Lucius cut off all their crystal shipments."

"Why?" Vanna queried.

"No one knows why but I need to get going before they really get suspicious." Pam sounded as if she was losing her patience with them.

"But we could be of more help out there with you," Cole protested.

Pam crossed her arms looking at him. "That defeats

the reason for us coming here. You wanted to find out who that person in your Stargazer was, you need to stay here and investigate."

Tia put her hand on Cole's arm as he opened his mouth. "She's right," Tia told him, "and you know it."

Cole frowned but closed his mouth and settled back silently.

Pam laughed. "Let's talk tonight." With a jaunty wave, she was gone.

"So, what now?" Chance asked, giving a short shrug holding out both hands.

"Now, he speaks up," Chad grumbled.

His brother snorted. "I know when to stay silent, you should take notes." He grinned and dodged the half-hearted punch his brother sent his way. "Missed."

"I guess we start researching." Telara moved between them before their small tussle turned into a full-blown altercation that could end up with damage.

"Where?" Tia leaned forward placing her chin on Telara's shoulder, not moving even when Telara moved her shoulders back.

"You guys look lost."

Zane's voice gave them all a jolt of surprise as they turned to see him standing there. Looking around they saw they were standing in the open with no buildings for any-one to come out from. Were they really that distracted they didn't see him coming? To the back of them was the sound of training coming from the training field but it was over ten yards away, surely, they would have seen him coming?

"No, not lost. Just..." Telara's voice trailed off as she looked at Zane and saw his lips twitching, seems they amused him.

"I got something to show you, if you guys are interested." He turned and walked away, not waiting for their response. They looked at each other, not sure how to react but decided they better catch up with him and see what he wanted to show them.

Could be what we've been looking for. Telara gave Vanna a small smile, always the mother hen wanting to give out reassurances.

Or another dead end.

Telara frowned at Chad. *How about some positive thinking.*

Chad shrugged. *I'm positive this could be another dead end?*

Telara glared at him but when he tripped over a root that just happened to appear above the ground, she couldn't stop the giggle that escaped.

Zane glanced back at them as he kept moving towards his office door, effectively silencing their amusement. "That's what happens when you don't pay attention to your surroundings."

They nodded in agreement with him just as they arrived at the hill that housed his quarters, pausing briefly to look at each other, realizing what he had just said. They need to quit being so obvious. Zane opened the door and motioned for them to follow him through. As they passed the door, they got a better view of the designs on the door. Telara's eyes widened as she saw eight symbols etched into the surface of the door, each of their powers being represented there. The eye for her power, the flame for Cole's, the wisps of wind for Tia, the leaf for Vanna, the lightning bolt for I.Q., a shard of ice for Chad and of course the waves of water for Chance. The eighth symbol she didn't recognize, it seemed to be several swirls moving around within the circle.

Telara stopped. *Tell me I'm not the only one seeing this.*

You're not the only one seeing it, Cole responded back to her, staring at the door and the moving symbols etched there.

Thank god. She swallowed hard. *So tired of being the only mental one here.*

"Are you guys coming?" Zane asked, turning around to look at them still staring at the door. "Or did you change your minds?"

"No, we didn't change our minds," Telara spoke slowly, pulling away from the door and still moving symbols. They moved through the doorway to follow Zane, having to jog slightly to catch up. Moving through the hallways they looked around in awe, passing openings in the hallway as well as more wooden doors that lead somewhere they couldn't see. The hallway they were walking down opened up into a circular room with a domed ceiling that was large enough to park several semis in. The room was empty except for the eight doors, each with one of the symbols from the door at the entrance.

They stood there looking around them at the doors that seemed to come alive around them. Flames danced across the surface of the door closest to the doorway they walked out of, more flames were climbing up the jambs before circling back down. It looked so real Telara was sure if anyone but Cole touched the door they would end up with severe burns.

The door with the swaying leaf seemed to sprout flowers and vines everywhere. The wood on the door rippled and creaked until it resembled the bark on a tree, Telara thought she even heard the squeak of a squirrel and wondered if Streak had somehow managed to follow them. Good thing all the doors were at least ten feet apart with this one being next to the fire door.

Icy film covered the following door, creating intricate designs of swirls and loops within the surface. Shards of ice rose from different spots on the door slab and jambs creating their own designs as well as a frigid rod like handle.

The sound of water had them each looking at the door next in line to see a waterfall flowing down the face of the door, pooling into a basin at the bottom but not once overflowing onto the floor below. The sounds of droplets pattering down the wooden jambs forming streams of water that disappeared into the wood.

A loud whistling could be heard from the next door as they stared at it, gusts of wind were blowing across the face, pulling up pieces of bark as it swirled around resembling a small windstorm beating at the door. The jamb looked battered as if it had just survived a tornado, which could be the case considering the windy storm raging across the face.

A loud snapping sound hurt their ears as well as several bright flashes that had them raising their hands to guard their eyes. The next door had jagged lines streaking down in multicolor fashion, creating its own lightning storm. Up and down the jambs were yellow lines and circles that were moving as well.

Telara gasped as she saw the next door, in the center was an eye that opened and closed but it was the designs that were moving around the door that had her attention. They were just like her friends from the ceiling in her room back home in their bungalow at Sanctuary. All the circles, lines and swirls moving quickly about in an erratic fashion.

The final door looked as if the wood had been dyed a dark black although it looked like it had dark shapes that were moving underneath the surface. Telara had figured out the other doors were related to their individual powers but this one had nothing to do with their powers, while she felt amazed and invigorated looking at the other doors, this one gave off an odd vibe that she couldn't describe.

Zane moved closer to them, blocking off her view of the dark door. She looked up at him but he was watching Cole as he moved closer to the fire door. She couldn't place the look on his face but it was almost like a proud parent or teacher, just different. She had been trying to decipher the look when he turned it on her. She looked away quickly, feeling her face grow warm at being caught staring at him.

"What is this place?"

She let out a breath of relief at I.Q.'s question.

Zane looked from her to him. "I call these rooms the Prime rooms."

CHAPTER 9

W hat are Prime rooms?" Chance looked over at the doors, his gaze moving to the waterfall as if drawn there and they possibly could've been.

"They are rooms where you can prime your powers," Zane told him with a smirk. "Hence, Prime rooms."

Chad's forehead furrowed. "Prime our powers? You mean train them?"

"In a manner." Zane agreed. "Yes!"

"Like our power room at home!" Cole exclaimed, eyes shining bright.

"In our bungalow at Sanctuary, we have a room called the power room that has all our elements there for us to practice our powers," I.Q. explained.

The expression on Zane's face went from mildly pleased to shuttered, something that seemed odd and out of place. "These rooms will put that one to shame, I can assure you of that."

"Why?"

Zane turned to look at Vanna at her question. "Excuse me?"

"Why would you have these rooms if you've never had any Guardians here?"

It didn't seem like Zane was going to answer her, he was silent for several moments before speaking up, "Who said we never had any Guardians here?"

"Wasn't something said about the Guardians not being allowed here when we first got here?" Telara frowned.

"Was there?" Zane grinned down at her. "I don't remember hearing anything like that." His gaze moved over each one of them before landing on Telara for a few moments before he gave a shrug and started to move back to the hallway. "Although if you would rather keep with your little power room back home, you're more than welcome."

His hand reached for the handle when Telara surprised herself and blurted out, "Actually we would like to check these out."

"Static!" Cole and Chad said in unison, gripping their fists and pulling their arms back sharply in an excited manner. The others laughed at their reactions.

Zane's husky laughter joined theirs. "Well then, let's prime up those powers of yours."

Cole looked over at the doors, then back at Zane. "What do we do?"

"I start by opening the door," Zane suggested.

"But how, only one has a handle?" Chance pointed to the door of ice where the ice rod shone brightly with the reflection of the flames that seemed to shine brighter as Cole moved closer to the door, examining the door, looking for a handle.

"Try getting closer." Zane watched Cole with that same look of affection from earlier. A look that seemed odd to Telara although Cole was too mesmerized by the door of flames.

Cole moved each closer to the door, the others in the room gasped as a fiery loop appeared, creating a pull on the door of pure flames. Zane watched as Cole reached out, grasping the pull with his left hand and pulling the door open.

Six sets of eyes looked around Cole to see into the room; what they saw inside had them all speechless. Cole moved slowly into the room with the others gingerly following, the room looked as if there was a whole different world inside. One with a blackened stone floor that resembled the pictures from their school books of islands where a volcano had erupted, hardened and cooled volcanic ash. As Cole moved across the terrain with ease, the others were touching the ground with the tips of their sneakers to make sure the ground wasn't still hot.

Zane's laughter had them turning around just as Telara finally stepped into the room. "I can promise you that there is nothing in these rooms that will hurt you, unless that's what you want."

"Not really," Tia told him, moving in after Telara, the others following until they were all in the desolate, blackened room staring around them. Zane was watching them with that same look on his face of affection, there had to be something behind it, Telara was sure of it even if she had no proof.

But Zane eyed Cole and not even looking at Telara. Turning to look at Cole she gave a tilt of her head as she watched him. Cole was holding out his hand towards a small lava pool, as they watched they saw flames rise from the pool and moved through the air, weaving its way towards Cole's hand. The flames circled his hand until you could barely see his hand beneath the flames. The flames grew brighter, shining so bright they could see the reflections in Cole's eyes.

They watched in awe, expecting to see his body covered in flames just like in Alaska, but as they watched Cole closed his hand and the flames were gone, snapping them out of their trance.

"What happened?" Chad looked at Cole who was staring at his closed fist but Cole didn't respond, didn't look away from his fist.

"Don't tell me you're going to let hothead get to you," Zane spoke from behind them. Cole tuned and looked at him but didn't say anything. "You've got the potential to be better than him and he knows it. You have talent while he's full of nothing but hot air; you've nothing to prove to him, only yourself."

Telara and the other Guardians looked back and forth between Zane, who watched Cole, and to Cole, who was still looking at his fist. They held their breath when Cole looked up from his fist to stare into Zane's eyes, not sure what Cole was going to do. To their surprise, Cole's fist burst into flames, flames that spread up his arm but stopped there. Zane smiled. "You might want to extinguish the flames if you want to see the other rooms though."

Cole looked down at his arm with satisfaction. The flames disappeared back down his arm into his closed fist, which he opened to show his empty palm.

"That's awesome, bro!" Chad ran up to him and clapped him on the shoulder with a big grin, then turned to look at Zane. "Will all our powers be this hyped up in our rooms?"

Zane lifted his shoulders slightly while spreading out his hands with a slight tilt of his lips. "I can't say for sure; these rooms don't enhance your powers, all they do is give you the freedom to use them in their own environment. It is up to you whether or not your powers bloom. Speaking of blooms," he looked over at Vanna whose eyes lit up, "ready to check out your room?"

She nodded, rushing out the room with everyone following.

Vanna was standing outside her door looking down at the branch that grew from the door and created a handle that she was now grasping and turning. Inside the room they saw a world of green foliage with shrubs and looming trees, Vanna moved into the room staring all around her with her mouth slightly gaped open. She casually toed off her shoes and then pulled off her socks so she could walk in the grass barefoot. With each step they saw flowers bloom where her foot lifted, creating footsteps of blooms.

"Whoa!" Chance breathed pointing to the footsteps. "Vanna, you are Mother Nature incarnate."

"This is better than the Mother Nature card in Crystal Paladins." Chad looked over at Cole, who was staring in wonder.

Chance snorted. "You are in the face of all this powerful magic that very few are privileged to see and you compare it to a card game?"

Chad shrugged, grinning at his brother. "Yup." Laughter filled the room but Chad turned to look at Zane. "My room is next, right?"

"I would put your shoes back on," I.Q. advised Vanna as they filed out to watch Chad grasp the ice rod that was already there.

"Brrrrr!" Tia wrapped her arms around herself shivering as they entered the icy world before them but Chad was already skidding across the ice shouting excitedly. Cole moved closer to her holding out his hands that started to glow, Tia moved her arms down as she felt the heat from Cole's hands. The others moved closer to them as Tia gave Cole a grateful smile.

Chad slid in the snow back to them coming to a sudden stop in front of them, spraying them with ice and snow. At the glares from his friends, he looked chagrined before glancing at Zane. "Maybe we should go to the next room, don't think they enjoy this environment as much as I do."

Zane laughed. "Not a bad call."

Chance moved to the door with the waterfall still flowing, as he got closer a round handle made of pure water appeared. He grasped it and turned, opening the door while the others held their breath, not sure what they were going to find behind the door. If it is a world of water, will it spill out into the room they were standing in?

Stepping inside they were standing on a smooth stone platform that overlooked a world of waterfalls, pools and a great big ocean. Chance kicked off his shoes and dived off the platform into the pool below, disappearing beneath the depths. They stood there for several moments before looking at each other not sure what to do next, none of them were great swimmers like Chance. Sure, they knew how to swim, well except for Vanna but still not enough to just go diving into an unknown pool.

"You might want to remind your friend that we still have more rooms to check out, unless he would rather stay here," Zane suggested with a grin that said he enjoyed this almost as much as them.

Hey bro! Chad hollered out via their mind link. *We're leaving with or without you.*

Vanna frowned at him but before she could say something Chance launched out of the pool on a gusher of water landing on the platform, spraying them with droplets of water laughing.

"Sorry." They laughed at his apology so he shook his head, spraying them more.

"Sure," his brother grumbled. "He sprays us and you laugh."

"Mine doesn't make our teeth chatter," his brother said, grabbing his shoulder and moving him outside the room so they could check out the next room. "Now let's go see this world of wind."

Tia stood in front of her door and took a deep breath before reaching out to the wind battered door, the pieces of wood that were flying around the face of the door moved to create a door handle for her. She pulled it open and stepped in with them following as they realized they were standing on a mountain cliff. Around them the wind whipped all around, in the distance they saw more mountains but none as big as the mammoth one they were standing on now.

Tia moved to the edge of the cliff reaching out, they held their breath hoping the wind didn't jerk her off the cliff. Zane told them they couldn't get hurt unless they wanted it, but what about accidents? Telara was poised to rush and grab her friend if need be but as they watched the wind that was whipping around them slowed so that it became a gentle breeze flowing on by. The wind started to move around Tia's outstretched hand like the flames back in Cole's room.

"This is too cool." Telara nodded in agreement with Chance's statement.

"You guys ready to move on to the next one?" Zane said, looking at I.Q., who had been silent but moved outside quickly at Zane's question.

Telara had to go grab Tia and pull her back. "C'mon, let's go see what I.Q.'s world looks like." Tia gave an absent nod but followed her.

I.Q. grasped a lightning rod hand and pushed on the door opening to a world that resembled a wasteland with lightning streaking across the sky, but there were also computer components strewn across the land. Some were actually complete computer systems but not all.

"Reminds me of one of those dystopian novels about a future where robots have taken over and destroyed humanity," Chad said, moving into the room. "Hey!" he protested when his brother jerked him back, then gasped as a lightning bolt hit the exact spot he was standing in. "Whoa!"

They looked at each other. "Telara's room."

Telara moved to the door and waited for a handle to appear but the eye just looked down at her while the shapes moved erratically across the face of the door. She looked back at everyone who stood there watching. She wasn't sure what she was supposed to do. How was she supposed to create a door handle, how did her friends do it?

It just appeared really, Tia told her and the others agreed with her. *I didn't do anything except move to the door and want to go in.*

Telara took a deep breath and moved forward, letting her feeling of wanting to go inside the room flow through her but still no handle. She frowned and looked back at Zane, he said nothing but nodded at her with an encouraging look as if to say he had faith in her. Letting out a breath, she turned back around and placed her hand on the door, willing it to open and let her in, which it did. She turned around with a big smile while her friends cheered and Zane looked proud.

Moving into the room, she frowned. No wasteland of fire, ice, air or electricity but also no field of flowers or water delights. She tentatively stepped forward, considering there was nothing there in front of her. When she stepped down there was a solid surface even though she couldn't see one, so she moved forward, walking on nothing. Turning around she saw her friends standing at the door, shaking their heads.

"I refuse to walk into a room where I can't see the floor," I.Q. told her, and she couldn't blame him. She looked at Zane.

"Why isn't there anything here?"

Zane grinned. "Your mind is blank until you fill it with knowledge, correct?" She nodded. "So fill this room with the knowledge that you want here with you. You can create your own reality."

She frowned, not sure what he meant but decided to attempt to fill this room. She breathed in and closed her eyes thinking about how nice it would be to have a floor in the room. She opened her eyes when she heard her friends gasp out, all around them was a floor.

CHAPTER 10

I created a whirlpool that was bigger than a whole football field," Chance was boasting as they left the hall of powers after Zane had come to tell them it was time for dinner. They had completely lost track of time as each of them played in their respective rooms. It wasn't like they didn't know how to work their powers, but they always had to dial them back so as not to do too much damage so they were all too scared to let them go.

"Yeah, well I built my own ice mansion *with* a place to sit," his brother gloated as he strutted along.

"You able to encase your body in ice and glide along on an ice slide through the air?" Cole grinned then laughed as Chad shoved at him.

Telara laughed with them during the walk towards the cafeteria bunker, they had all been making incredible progress with their powers and worked up an appetite they hadn't even realized. Telara had made the floor to walk on although she hadn't done much more in the room except create a sofa to sit where she just stared around her. Her power wasn't creating material things out of thin air, so she wasn't sure what she had learned today but she didn't want to dampen her friend's enthusiasm so she just listened.

They were moving through the food line when Chance turned to her. "You're awful quiet, how was your time in your Prime room? Making anything other than a floor appear?"

She reached for a slice of pizza, salad and a can of soda before opening her mouth, "I did." She moved towards the table where Tia and Vanna were already seated talking animatedly about their experiences.

"Well?" Cole sat next to her with a plate full of spaghetti.

Before she could answer, Pam sat down with them. She tried to repress the feeling of thankfulness she felt, although from the narrowed look from Tia, she knew Tia could sense her feelings. The others, thankfully, were too engrossed about their experiences.

"El capitán." Cole lifted his can up in salute.

Pam shook her head, taking a bite from her salad. "You guys seem to be in high spirits."

"It has been a good day," Vanna said, popping a slice of cucumber into her mouth. "I was able to create some pretty cool floral statues today with just a thought."

Pam looked thoughtfully, watching them.

"I flew." Tia spoke with a beaming look of pride as she took a big bite out of her Italian sub. At Pam's raised brow she went on to explain, "I learned how to ride the big gusts of winds in my Prime room."

"Prime room?" Pam looked curiously between them all.

"That is what Zane calls them," Cole spoke up, forking a meatball and taking a big bite.

Pam's brow furrowed as she looked over at Telara, "Huh?"

"In Zane's barracks he has some rooms he calls the Prime rooms where we're able to train or prime our powers." Telara told her.

"So did he tell you anything about the past Guardian?" Pam asked and each of their faces fell as they realized they hadn't asked Zane about that.

They looked over at each other, those who had been shoveling food in their mouths were now swallowing hard. Telara looked up with a chagrined look. "We got so caught up with practicing our powers that we kinda forgot to ask."

Pam gave a half chuckle as she took another drink. "I don't blame you, I would've gotten distracted as well." They gave a sigh of relief before she continued, "Just don't forget about why we came here in the first place."

Telara nodded. "We won't."

"So, how did your patrol go? Find any of the lost Arions?" I.Q. asked her.

Pam gave a shake of her head. "None of them, something is going on but I'm not sure exactly what."

"So, what are you going to do?" Tia looked at her.

"I don't know yet." Pam looked at her food, in deep thought.

"Maybe we can talk to Zane and see what he knows about the disappearances," Telara suggested but Pam shook her head.

"No, I'll find out what is going on."

"What makes you think something is going on?" Telara asked her.

"They are all acting odd," Pam told them. "As if they

are hiding something. Avoiding my questions and trying to distract me."

"What are you going to do about it?" Chance asked her.

Pam looked up at him. "I plan to find out what is going on."

"How?" Telara asked her.

"Let me worry about that," Pam told her. "You just worry about finding out about that past Guardian." She rose from her seat. "Then we can head back home and hopefully figure out more of the mysteries that you've been facing."

Seated on the concrete benches around the Coliseum they watched as the performers took their places on the stage. There down on the stage was the blonde from last night, the man who rescued her standing next to her, his head held up high. There were others there as well, they must have been the ones from the secret meeting. They were standing up to defend a family against the dark soldiers who were attempting to arrest them, no known reason but after the play last night they were sure it wasn't for a legit reason.

They watched as the eight rebels took down the soldiers and freed the family who they helped to escape the town into the rebel camp that was hidden within the earth where the Supreme Ruler couldn't find them. They watched as the rebels grew in numbers, protecting those who couldn't protect themselves. They made many contacts throughout the land, but they still couldn't figure out what the Supreme Ruler wanted with those she took to her palace.

The days passed on the stage in front of them, the

rebels working against the Supreme Ruler to protect the citizens of their home and end the rule of the Supreme Ruler. The rebels grew day by day until they were their own army. Then came the day when a woman whose skin shone with multiple colors walked down the underground steps into the rebel's world as if she had a personal invitation. She walked into the room of the rebel leaders where they were planning a raid of the Supreme Ruler's armory.

They turned in surprise, picking up their weapons of metal. She shook her head at them. "You don't need your weapons, none of you will ever need them again."

"What do you mean?" The blonde looked from the woman to her allies standing with her.

"I can tell you what the woman who calls herself the Supreme Ruler wants, I can tell you why she is taking the ones from their families and keeping them in her palace where they are no better than the prisoners in her dungeon, and even better, I can tell you how to defeat her."

Telara and the other Guardians watched the story, holding their breath as they waited to hear more. They couldn't wait to see the Supreme Ruler being taken down by the rebels.

"But only if you do something for me first," the woman told them, pulling a groan from the Guardians, who slumped back in their seats.

"What is it that you want us to do?" the blond asked her.

"I need you to free one of her prisoners that is being held in her personal quarters."

"Why should we do that?" the rebel with the gruff demeanor demanded.

"Because she will be the one who helps us defeat the Supreme Ruler."

The stage went dark, signaling the end of the play. The players moved to the center of the stage and took their bows.

The sound of humming woke Telara from her sleep but she kept her eyes closed as she listened. The humming was indeed feminine which meant no dream visit from Zach but most likely another dream just like the first. The sound of glass clinking had her rolling over in her bed and opening her eyes. There were the same dressers and nightstands from before, just beyond the filmy curtains around the bed.

Taking a deep breath, Telara swung her legs over the side of the bed and stood up as she looked around. She walked the same path as before, and came to the same door as before. She peered into the room, just a bit more than before. She saw the same hand, reaching for the bottles on the shelves. Grabbing a small crystal bottle of pink crystal dust, she tilted the bottle and poured the glittering dust into a small crystal bowl. Another bottle was pulled down from the shelves as her slender fingers reached for crystal chips from the rounded bottle. Telara watched as the woman dropped a green, yellow and purple crystal chip into the same bowl.

"It's bad manners to lurk in doorways," the woman spoke so softly that Telara could barely tell the difference from her speaking to her humming. It took her a few moments to realize the woman was speaking to her. It had her halting in the doorway, unsure of her next actions.

The woman pulled a small bottle from her bracelet, a bottle that looked to be full of liquid, shimmering liquid that she poured into the small crystal bowl. Three drops of the sea blue liquid dropped into the bowl, creating a boiling liquid that released steam and a shimmering opaque cloud that hovered above the bowl.

The woman turned to smile at her, which had Telara standing still, her body tense as she looked into the completely white eyes with purple shards. "Hello Telara," the woman spoke softly, to Telara's surprise. Looking into her face Telara realized that the woman's skin was porcelain white in color, with some purplish hue. Her hair was a deep purple that fell in waves about her face.

"How do you know my name?"

The woman's smile seemed to widen. "here is much I know while there is little that you know."

Telara gave a grunt. "Tell me something I don't know."

"My child, I could tell you many things you don't know but that doesn't mean they will help you until you are able to understand them," the woman spoke with the same soft voice, her expression unchanging.

"So, why am I here?" Telara asked her. "And where is Zach?"

This time the woman's expression changed, her head tilted just slightly as she looked at Telara. "Who is Zach?"

"He's the one I normally see in my dreams."

"Dreams?" The woman watched her.

"Where we are now, I'm dreaming," Telara explained, starting to feel confused.

"Is that what you think?" the woman queried, her voice full of amusement.

Telara opened her mouth to speak up but closed it just as quickly, unsure of what to say. After all, did she know where she was? She closed her eyes in her bed and woke up here but does that mean she was sleeping like she was with Zach? She chewed on her bottom lip looking around her before turning back to look at the woman. "So, where am I?"

"Time to get going, Telly," Tia's voice broke through her dreams. There above her was Tia who was grinning down at her. "Let's go see Pam before she leaves."

Telara rolled over in her bed to see Vanna sliding her feet into her sneakers before she moved out of their room with Tia following her. "Turry up, Telly."

CHAPTER 11

S till no Zach?" Chance frowned at her while they ate
breakfast. When they got down Pam had already left
with Reggie for another patrol to discover what they
could about the disappearances.

Telara gave a solemn shake of her head staring down
at her barely eaten oatmeal; she didn't seem to have an
appetite this morning. Too much on her mind and none
of it made much sense right now. Lifting her spoon, she
watched the oatmeal slowly dribble down to drop with
a plop into the rest of the oatmeal in her bowl.

"But you said you spoke with the woman this time."
Tia tilted her head, looking at Telara who was still staring at the dribbling oatmeal.

"I did." Telara sighed, dropping her spoon into the
bowl, watching the oatmeal splatter over her shirt and
the table.

Vanna handed her a napkin. "What did she say?"

"She called me by name and told me there was a lot
that we didn't know." Telara's tone spoke volumes, volumes Cole validated with one sentence.

"As if we didn't already know that."

The others nodded in agreement, wearing the same sardonic expression.

"Forget this!" Chance stood up quickly, almost unseating his brother, who frowned at him. "Enough sitting around feeling all frumpy, we have our very own rooms waiting for us over in Zane's barracks. Let's go!"

"Yeah!" Everyone jumped up, excited to be able to play with their powers with freedom.

Telara rose, although slower than the others, and her feet seemed to drag as she followed them from the cafeteria to the brightness of the outside. Unlike the others, she didn't have the greatest experience in the Prime rooms. Sure, she made things appear in the room, enough to make it so that it wasn't completely empty. Couch, chair and even some wall decorations but that wasn't what her powers were. She wasn't even truly sure what she was supposed to be doing; how did you practice the power of the mind?

Watching the others trotting ahead of her, excited for the Prime rooms, she couldn't quell the little bit of jealousy that reared its ugly head. Their powers seemed so much easier for them to play around with in the rooms, their rooms which were tailored around their powers. How do you tailor a room around a power you can't see?

"Having issues?"

Telara jerked around quickly, almost falling off the small couch she had created in her room, to see Zane standing there smiling at her by the doorway. "Ever think of knocking?" she grumbled but he only laughed.

"Sorry, not used to having Guardians here in these rooms." He looked around the room then back at her. "I can leave if you would rather," he offered.

"No, you're right, I am having issues." Telara sighed, feeling the jerk for snapping at him over something that wasn't even his fault.

Zane moved further into the room and sat down on a small wooden chair that suddenly appeared. Telara frowned at the chair, she hadn't conjured it but there it was. Zane chuckled at her look of consternation. "Each Prime room works to appease the occupants of said room, I just know better than most on how to work it."

Telara pulled her feet up off the floor and underneath her as she studied him, then something he said clicked. "How do these rooms work?"

"With Prime crystals," he said simply.

"But you said Sanctuary won't send you any crystals, that they only give you the bare minimum." Telara leaned back.

Zane gave a small smile. "What Lucius and Ira don't know, won't cause me any problems." He watched her. "Unless you plan to tell them about it when you get back."

Telara scoffed. "As if I would tell them anything, they like holding stuff from me, I surely won't feel bad about holding something from them." She enjoyed hearing Zane's laughter, "besides, this has nothing to do with them."

Zane gave an appreciative smile. "The crystals work with powers to create an atmosphere of a certain power, the Prime crystals that power these rooms were already primed with existing powers that just so happened to coincide with yours."

"So, there are Prime crystals that are blank then?" Telara felt her curiosity rise as Zane nodded. "Can I see one?"

"That could be a possibility." Zane nodded again. "Learning more here than you did at Sanctuary?" Zane suggested when she seemed to go quiet, to which she gave a small shrug.

"The others are," she half mumbled, unable to look him in the eye.

"You're not learning anything new?" There was no censor or accusation in his voice.

Telara looked around the room. "Not really sure what I should be doing, honestly. I don't even really understand my power, my Crim works with it wonderfully during battles but when I try to think about what to do, my powers seem to freeze."

Zane inclined his head. "I understand that."

Her brow furrowed. "You understand?"

Zane gave an understanding smile, "kind of like when you study for a test and feel like you know everything until the test is put in front of you, then everything disappears as if you never studied at all."

"Yes!" Telara felt relieved to have it explained so simply but then her face fell, "so, how do I get around it?"

"You're putting your powers in a box and so they are rebelling," he told her.

Telara gave a jerky shake of her head. "My powers are rebelling because I'm putting them in a box?" When he nodded, she continued, "How am I putting them in a box?"

"Your powers are mental powers," Zane told her. "You're confining them just to that, either telepathy or telekinesis."

"Isn't that what mental powers are called?" Telara was starting to get confused.

Zane explained, "But that isn't all, you can do so much more, you are so much more." At Telara's look of confusion he continued, "the mind is a very powerful source, there isn't much that can't be done with the power of your mind. The energy all around you is yours to command if you wish. Relying too much on your Crim is holding you back from your true potential, use the Crim as it was meant to be used, as an extension and nothing more."

Telara looked around the room trying to figure out what he meant, she really wanted to show him that she could do it and had what it took to be the leader of the Guardians but she was confused.

Zane seemed to take pity on her. "You can use your mind to levitate objects, speak to your friends mentally so as not to let anyone else here but you can also read minds, control those more weak-minded than you as well as manipulate situations around you. Your power isn't only limited to your mind, you can create as well." Telara's eyes went wide at his words. She wasn't sure she liked the idea of reading minds or manipulating others, but she really wanted to expand her powers. "You just have to stop limiting yourself, let your powers run free and ride along with them."

Telara looked around her, biting her lip as she stood up and moved cautiously to the center of the room. As she moved the room around her disappeared as she thought about starting over, all around her was a darkness with sparkles far in the distance. It felt as if she was in space, although she had never been there and she could breathe as if she was standing outside in the sun with her toes curling in the grass. Looking down she saw that her feet were flat on the floor but pointed down as there was nothing there for them to stand on but she was holding herself there.

With just a thought she felt herself rise even more, she turned with a grin to see the expression on Zane's face but he was no longer there. She looked around, worried she had sent him falling to his doom but saw nothing but the sparkling darkness. Closing her eyes, she let her senses flow out to make sure that he was nowhere in the room, when the only presence she felt was her own, she went back to exploring more of her powers. Turning back around she did her best to not think about how to do something and just let it happen. She wanted to fly like Tia was talking about, she lifted even more so and moved around the darkness, leveling her body she went Superman mode and flew. She even clenched her right hand in a fist, holding it out ahead of her while the left hand clenched in a fist but held against her side.

She wasn't sure how long she flew but when she grew tired of flying, she spun around and thought of the water world where Chance ruled. The water seemed to flow all around her, filling up the void. As it rushed to encase her, she thought about an invisible field protecting her from the waves and there it was all around her. She pushed back against the water with her mind and created waves that splashed against the force field protecting her. Making a sweeping motion with her arms, the waves parted and disappeared.

She created a surface several feet below her, lowering her body down until her feet touched the solid ground.

She took off at a run, laughing as her feet barely touched the solid surface that kept extending itself out in front of her so that she always had something to run on. It was such a freeing feeling to just let it happen, not think about it but just let it happen. She would leap from the surface and let herself ride the energy all around her, letting it pick her up so that she was flying through the air. Not once did she even think to use the Crim on her hand, all the power came from her.

CHAPTER 12

You still haven't asked about the past Guardian?" Pam stared at them, her lips starting to tighten showing her irritation with what they just said. "I get the first night and even excused it but seriously?" She shook her head in frustration. "Why are we even here if all you guys are going to do is have fun? We need information."

They looked down, standing on the outside of the Coliseum after dinner. Pam had just gotten back from patrol with Reggie, who didn't even say hi to them as he walked past. They were so excited to tell Pam about how their powers felt as if they were improving and it was only two days.

Pam looked at Telara who had been so excited to finally speak about her powers improving to Pam. "You had Zane in a one-on-one conversation and not once thought to ask if they had any information on past Guardians?"

"Pam, that's not fair," Tia defended Telara, who felt her throat tighten so much that she couldn't speak.

Pam turned to look at her. "No, what's not fair is that you guys are goofing off while I'm out there in the field trying to figure out what is going on. I would love to play as well but I'm actually doing what we came here for."

Cole lifted his head, "Speaking of that, did you figure out what was giving you the feeling of things being off?"

"No." Pam turned to him. "But not because I wasn't trying." She ran a frustrated hand over her face. "You know what?" She held her hands up. "It doesn't matter, do what you want, it's only your lives I've been trying to save." With those harsh words, she turned on her heel and stormed off the same way Reggie had gone.

They saw Zane watching them with narrowed eyes, they turned and walked down the hill into the Coliseum, finding seating away from the others to watch the play of the night.

"Zane put you in time out?" They looked up to see Billy sitting down on a bench right above them. They hadn't even noticed him when they sat down.

Telara frowned at him. "We don't need your pity."

Billy leaned back on the bench, his elbows resting on the bench on the next level behind him. "I don't waste my time on pity, you guys just happen to be in my seat."

Looking at each other, they shared the same look of consternation as they tried to remember if they saw where he sat during the other shows. Vanna looked at him with narrowed eyes. "This is a big Coliseum, I'm sure there are plenty of other seats."

Not once did Billy look their way, his gaze on the stage where the performers were getting everything set up for the next installment. "None like the seats over here."

Telara stared at him for a few moments before shaking her head, looking up as his sister walked up, twirling a pen on a chain around her finger. "Whatcha sitting over here for?" she asked her brother, causing the others to look at him with raised brows, which he just ignored.

He gave his sister a dark look. "You can be replaced, you know."

"Nope!" His sister sat next to him still twirling the pen. "One of a kind."

"The painful kind maybe." His voice sounded irritated but they could also see that he truly cared for his sister, under the gruffness that he wore like armor.

Telara looked around them but couldn't see Pam anywhere.

"Looking for someone?" Billie leaned down, tilting her head to look at Telara who just shook her head. The music from the stage saved her from any more questions as tonight's performance started.

They watched as the rebels broke into the palace and rescued the prisoner, a small petite little girl with big eyes who barely spoke while they smuggled her from the palace. The anger from the Supreme Ruler was vicious, many of her soldiers met their death that night.

Over the next few days they had fallen into a routine, each morning they would rise and head to breakfast where they would eat, sometimes alone and sometimes they would have company. Billy joined them a few times with his familiar smirk and green mohawk although they never saw his sister once. Billy told them that she worked in the office during the mornings.

"Administration like Lucy?" Cole asked.

Billy nodded and grumbled, "those two are friends."

"What's wrong with that?" Vanna looked over at him with a frown.

"Nothing." He shrugged. "When they aren't ganging up on me."

Tia laughed. "I'm betting you deserve it."

Telara did her best to hide her smirk at the dark look Billy threw Tia. They saw Logan as well, even though he kept his distance from Vanna, much to Billy's amusement, but not once did they see Pam at breakfast, not even a glimpse of her. After breakfast they headed straight to the Prime rooms, there they practiced their powers that seemed to grow with each day. Ice castles, bridges and sculptures littered Chad's room, Cole could submerge himself into lava without any damage to himself, Vanna's room was like a forest along with animals that she could have conversations with, I.Q. boasted of creating an energy being that became his assistant he called Sarah, Tia spent most of her time in the air although she was excited to tell them about the tornado she created, as much time as Chance spent under the water you would think he would be a permanent prune.

Telara loved levitating herself, flipping around in the air as she felt like a superhero flying around. With just a thought her room would go from outer space to a room with furniture but mostly she just liked the feeling of being free from everything while she floated around in space.

From the Prime rooms they would go have dinner, no Pam still, then check out the play for the night. The prisoner the rebels rescued told them that the Supreme Ruler wanted her because of visions that she saw, also told of a prisoner who could tell of prophecies but that she was sure that one was dead. Told how they were all from a land called Malonia, all with special talents that the Supreme Ruler coveted so that she could achieve her nefarious plan.

"What plan?" the leader of the rebels asked her.

"She plans to combine the three crystals and take the power from the Keeper." At their blank stares, the girl continued, "If she succeeds, she will have the power to create and destroy worlds." The rebels blanched at her words.

"How do we stop her?" the tall man next to the rebel leader asked.

"I will help you, teach you what you need to know, teach you the forgotten arts of crystal magic," the girl told them. Over the next few nights each play would document the girl teaching the rebels all about the crystals that their world was created from. Told how they were taken from the people by the original overlords who had taken over their realm and enslaved the people, the parent's of the Supreme Ruler. They had taken away the knowledge of the crystals and their creators. The rebels learned that some of them were descendants of great warriors called the Paladins, that they had great powers the Supreme Ruler couldn't control which was why she hid the knowledge of such. They watched as some of the rebels learned to use fire, water, earth, air, electricity, ice, mind and even emotions.

Then would come the dreams, each night Telara would wake in that bed with the curtains surrounding the bed, see the crystal figurines on the dresser and walk to the doorway where she would see the slender figure standing in the small room where the different types of vials lined the shelves and littered the top of the table along with small crystals as well metal utensils the woman would use as she hummed to herself while working. Telara had no idea what she was working on, she hadn't said a word to Telara since that night and each time Telara moved into the room she would wake up.

Usually, Telara would fly around the vast nothingness of space in her room but when Zane entered her room, he found her laying on her stomach, staring out the window of the room she created.

"Penny for your thoughts?"

Telara wasn't startled by his question, sure, she had been lost in thought staring out the window she created but she had also felt his presence before he entered. It was weird, she could sense everything in the room and outside as well. Putting her hands on the floor, she pushed herself off the floor to sit up with her legs crossed as she looked over at Zane who held out a sandwich to her.

"I noticed that all of you seem to miss lunch, thought maybe I would rectify that today." Sitting down in one of the wooden chairs with blue cushions he watched her take the sandwich silently. "Care to talk about it?" he asked.

Unwrapping the sandwich, she grinned seeing it was a mayonnaise and pickle sandwich, a treat she had loved as a child but couldn't remember the last time she had eaten one. Taking a big bite, she closed her eyes as the flavor from her youth exploded in her mouth. She wasn't sure if she would still enjoy it when she took that first bite but now, she knew, it was still good. "Thank you for the sandwich." She looked up at him leaning back up against the couch that matched the wooden chair.

Zane spoke carefully as he watched her. "If you don't want to talk about it, you don't have to."

"About what?" She looked up at him sideways.

"Why you were staring off into space as if you were lost with no life jacket."

She gave a halfhearted chuckle at his words. "That's one way to put it." She gave a sigh. "Not sure really, I mean we've never been able to work our powers like we have since you showed us these rooms. It's been awesome."

"But..." he prompted.

"I still feel like I'm behind, that I should be doing more than what I'm doing." She looked down at her Rotary, then back up at him. "The others all are doing spectacular things with their powers and while I'm doing more than I was ..." She trailed off.

"You still feel like something is missing," he finished for her and she nodded. He stood up and held out his hand to her, she stared at it for a few seconds before placing her hand inside of his. He lifted her off the floor and led her to the center of the room. "Did anyone tell you that you are the first Guardian with the power of the mind since the beginning?"

She shook her head slowly. "I don't think so."

He gave a disgruntled sound as he gave a shake of his head. "They fear the power of the mind."

This Telara wasn't expecting. "Why?"

He gave her an incredulous look. "You really don't know?" She shook her head. "There is nothing more powerful than the mind, there isn't anything you can't do." He chuckled at her cynical look. "You don't believe me."

She responded, "I don't really feel all that powerful."

"That isn't your fault," he told her. "I'm sure Lucius and the others at Sanctuary felt safer if they suppressed your power rather than let you live up to your potential."

"What is my potential?" she asked.

"Whatever you want it to be," he told her.

This time she snorted. "Now you sound like Lucius."

"I'm nothing like him." Gone were the jovial grins and friendly gleam in his eyes. Now his voice was harsh as his look hardened.

"Sorry." She stepped back, feeling bad that she upset him. Lucius made her mad as well but his voice and look made her feel as if whatever he had against Lucius, it went deep. "I didn't mean it as an insult."

"I know you didn't," he quickly assured her, his hard looks softening slowly. "That's all right, it's not your fault."

"Can I ask why you don't like him?"

"Long story," he told her. "Maybe I'll tell you about it sometime but for now, let's work on taking your powers from something missing to nothing left to hide."

She took a deep breath and gave a sharp dip of her head. "I'm ready!"

He laughed and it made her feel so much happier to know he wasn't upset anymore; she wasn't sure what made him so likable but she wondered if there was a possibility of them staying there to finish their training. She bet with Zane as a teacher they would have more of a chance with the Magine and Shadow Master.

"When you read a book, can you imagine the story

in your mind?" he asked her. She nodded. "That is the power of the mind, is it not?" This time the nod was a bit hesitant as she tried to figure out where he was going with this. He breathed out as his face screwed up into a thoughtful look, he even brought his fingers up to softly grasp his chin as his pointer finger tapped his chin looking around. Then he looked back at her. "Tell me about the last book you read."

Telara paused thinking about the question. "*Child of the Dragon*." She told him. "It was about a child who grew up in a small village who was an orphan that was hunted by some ugly looking creatures called Circs when he turned 16. Come to find out he was the child of the Dragon Lord, cursed at birth to live his life as a child to punish the Dragon Lord."

"What did the Dragon Lord look like?" Zane asked her.

Telara thought really hard. "He was almost as large as a mountain, dark scales the color of the night with eyes golden yellow and when his wings were outstretched, they could cover a football field. On his massive chest was a scar where the Circs had tried to carve out his heart; they failed but they left a scar that resembled a fox." She laughed thinking about how weird that sounded to her when she read it. "He would rear his head back and let out a roar so loud that the ground would shake with the sound as the air burned with the fire he would breathe out."

"Roooaarrrr!" The sound of a big beast bellowing had her stumbling and falling at Zane's feet, he helped her to stand up, pointing at the dark black dragon that loomed above them. The exact dragon she had just imagined, his head rearing back letting loose the stream of fire she had described.

Pulling her astonished gaze from the dragon she looked at Zane. "Where did he come from?"

He laughed and tapped her nose. "You."

"Me?" she squeaked.

He grinned. "You."

Turning around she let out another squeak as the dragon stared at her, she wasn't sure where the courage she had when confronting Kull the dragon but right now her body was so tense it hurt. To be fair, this dragon was much larger than Kull. "How do I get rid of it?" she asked, taking a step back.

"The same way you conjured him," Zane told her, as if that answer was all it took.

"That's good," her voice betrayed her nervousness, "would be even better if I knew how I did it." Her tongue darted out nervously to wet her lips.

"You can do this, you brought him to life with your descriptions and your imagination." Zane's voice was right next to her ear as he spoke. "Now you just need to un-imagine him."

"Un-imagine him," Telara said, swallowing hard. "Sure, no problem." She took a deep breath as the drag-on looked down at her, slowly lowering its head towards her. She closed her eyes silently telling the dragon to go back to the book. When she opened her eyes, she yelled out, right in front of her were two yellow eyes staring at her.

Zane let out a bark of laughter. "Unless you are want-ing to keep him as a pet, if so, just know that you are in charge of cleaning up after him."

Telara forgot about the dragon that was right in front of her as she turned to stare at Zane, astonished that he was joking about this. "I'm not cleaning up after no thousand-pound lizard!" She turned to see the dragon giving her a curious look. "Time for you to go home!" she told him, mentally enforcing the banishment and as she watched, the dragon blurred from sight before he was gone. She grinned as she turned to look at Zane, jumping up and down in excitement. "I did it! He's gone!"

"Yes, you did." He stared at her, his look reminding her of how her dad would smile proudly at her when she accomplished a goal. "Now, time to see what else you can do."

CHAPTER 13

Telara moved cautiously towards the vision she created; it was something Vanna would have approved of, a cuddly furry creature the size of a puppy with big eyes smiling up at her with puffy lips and purple fur that has sprigs of yellow sticking out. She gasped when she felt the softness of the fur beneath her fingers, giggled when the creature tilted its cute little head. "You're such a cutie," she tickled his chin. "Vanna would be so jealous right now. What should I call you?" she pondered as she scratched his ears, causing his hind leg to thump on the ground.

As she pondered, she thought about a movie she had seen when she was younger about a boy who had gone to another planet where there were some cute critters there as well. Except for the fact that when he got to close their mouths grew larger with knife-like fangs that almost ate the child.

"Hey!" she shouted as Zane pulled her back quickly, frowning at him momentarily she shrieked and almost climbed up him when she saw the cute little critter had turned into the evil creatures from the movie she was just thinking of. "No!" she shouted pointing at the creature that was growling and advancing on them both. "Go away!" she ordered, stomping her foot. With a pop the creature was gone and she sighed in relief, then gave Zane a chagrined look. "Sorry."

He just laughed and ruffled her hair. "Not a problem, just be careful with your thoughts when you are projecting them like that."

"I can't wait to show the others what I can do." She bounced a bit on the balls of her feet. "They will be so geeked." The grin that spread across her face felt almost as if it was stuck there, she couldn't stop smiling. She looked over at Zane, hoping he didn't think she was a complete idiot but he looked as happy as she felt. "Is there anything else that I can do?"

"That is up to you, your only limitations are those that you set upon yourself," he told her, then chuckled at the frown that appeared. "Before you compare me to someone that I would rather not be compared to, let me explain." He watched her and when she stayed silent, with a small smile as she watched him as if she was amused by the fact that he knew what she was thinking, he continued, "Powers aren't as simple as this person can create a flame and that person can talk to animals. The past Guardians were only ever trained at Sanctuary and for one purpose, a purpose that they relied more on crystal weapons than actual powers. Trained by one person who taught them how to go out and die to appease Gods and Goddesses who no longer matter."

With jerky movements Zane moved away from her walking around the room that Telara had created, his hands moving over the surface of the wooden dragon bench, grinning when the purple and yellow polka dotted bird landed on his arm. "Each power is special to the person who wields it, there are possibilities but it depends on the person as to whether they will be able to accomplish them," he looked over at her. "Or even surpass them and become more. What I'm trying to say is not to limit yourself to what anyone, including me, tell you that you can do."

"Okay … but some nudge in the right direction could be helpful," she suggested, looking up at him, enjoying hearing his hearty laughter filled the room.

"Okay, okay." Still laughing, he continued. "You got it, nudges."

She gave a triumphant look, rocking back on the balls of her feet with her thumbs hooked into the belt loops of her jeans. "So, what's next, teach?"

Zane looked around the room at all the illusions that Telara had created, then looked back at her, "You can bring your thoughts alive around you, now can you project your thoughts into the mind of others?"

"Me and the others do it all the time," she started to protest but stopped at the shake of his head.

"You guys have a tight connection, one that no other Guardian had, and one so powerful that you guys can communicate with each other without thinking about it." He watched her try to process what he was saying. "You guys are communicating but what I'm talking about is projecting your thoughts, what you are seeing into another's mind. Someone other than another Guardian."

"How would I do that?"

He gestured around them. "The same way you projected these visions to the outside."

"I don't know if I could do that to someone." She fidgeted, looking anywhere but at him. "Who would I do that to?"

"Me."

She jerked around to stare at him, her eyes wide while he stood there watching her with that smile of his. "Are you crazy? You're willing to let a novice inside your head?"

He moved closer to her and placed his hands on her shoulders. "I have faith in you, now you just need to have faith in yourself." She looked up at him, chewing on her lips. "You can do this."

"I don't know how." Her voice was so low she wasn't sure he heard her, wasn't sure she wanted him to hear her as she lowered her gaze.

He lifted up her chin, making her look into his eyes. "All you have to do is think of something and then push that vision into my mind. You can do this, you won't hurt me, I promise."

She took a shaky breath. "You sure?"

"Yes." He released her chin and moved to take her hands in his, placing them on the side of his head. "Let me see what's going on in that pretty little head of yours." He released her hands, letting his hang down as his smiling eyes looked into hers.

This time the breath she breathed in was a bit more stable. Her fingers pressed deeper into his hair feeling his scalp beneath them. Closing her eyes she let her thoughts flow, thinking of the time her and her sister were in the store to get a dress for their cousin's wedding. A song by the Couch Loafers came over the store's speaker system and she started to dance to it in the middle of the aisle, completely embarrassing her sister. Zane chuckled at the vision that he was seeing, she couldn't blame him, she wasn't the best dancer around.

Next, she thought of the rest of her family, her big brother who had joined the Air Force right out of high school, the last time they had seen him was at his Air Force graduation. The look of pride on her parent's faces when they watched him walk across the runway. Her father and her laughing as they attempted to avoid being in pictures that her mother was attempting to take. Her mother had almost gotten her in one when her father swung her around so her mother only got a picture of her father's back. The laughter of her, her twin sister Ra, big brother and her father drowning out the grumblings of her mother. The vision disappeared as Zane jerked away from her, she wasn't sure how but she could feel his aggravation, possibly because of the connection of her showing him the visions. "I'm sorry," she apologized although she wasn't sure what she had done.

"It's not you," he was quick to assure her. "It was just a bit overwhelming." He gave a tight smile.

"How about something else?" she suggested, rocking on her feet.

"Maybe next time," he said, his smile still not the relaxed she was used to seeing. "I forgot about an appointment I can't be late for." He shot her a wink as he headed towards the door. "You should probably think about wrapping it up soon as well, almost dinner time." With that he was gone and she was standing there with all the illusions she had created slowly dissipating around her.

"Who needs an illusion crystal when we have Telly?" Cole quipped as they left the cafeteria, they had been discussing their time in the rooms as they always did although this time she had much more to tell. They were all eager to hear about her experience, Chad couldn't get past the part about her projecting her thoughts into Zane's mind.

"Can you do that to me?" The excitement in his voice was infectious, but his words had her flashing back to Zane's agitation. She still wasn't sure what had brought that on, she hadn't been feeling any agitation at the time. She remembered that day and knew it was a day the whole family was in a good mood. She never got to show him the ice cream parlor they had visited afterwards.

"I still need to control it more." She shook her head at him as they moved towards the Coliseum, Zane's reaction was still fresh in her mind. As they started down the dirt steps of the Coliseum, she looked around for Zane but didn't see him anywhere, which was unusual, she didn't think he missed any of the shows.

They found some seats next to Billy, Billie and Lucas. Billie and Lucas smiled at them but Billy just stared straight ahead at the stage, his brown loafers resting against the bench in front of him as he leaned back against the bench behind him, his elbows resting along that bench as well.

"Comfortable?" He turned, facing Telara, his dark brow rising at her question.

"Problem?"

Telara shook her head at his question. "Nope, but I do have a question for you." He watched her but said nothing so she continued, "Why dye your hair green but not your brows? They're still dark."

116

"I could ask the same of you." He turned back towards the stage leaving her staring at him dumbfounded."

"My hair isn't colored," she protested.

He snorted. "Sure it isn't."

Before she could argue with him anymore, the lights from the stage started flashing, she turned away from him to look at the stage but not before she shot him a glaring look. She really wanted to pluck each and every one of those spiky green strands of hair out of his head. They watched as the rebels rose up against the Supreme Ruler, using their newfound powers against her and her soldiers. They defeated the soldiers but the Supreme Ruler created a portal and disappeared through it before they could apprehend her. At the guidance of the one who helped them with their powers and the knowledge of what the Supreme Ruler was after, they followed her through the portal.

The stage went dark as the play ended.

CHAPTER 14

W ell hello," the soft voice startled Telara, who jerked around astonished to see the woman from her dreams standing before her. She looked around realizing she was no longer asleep in her room but was indeed in the dream bedroom she always wakes up in. Although normally, she would wake up alone in the room, this was the first time the woman had left her room with all the vials and crystals.

"Ummm…hello." Telara hated the hesitancy in her voice but she wasn't truly sure what was going on this time. The woman had only spoken to her once before but since that night, nothing.

The woman gave a gentle nod of her head and gestured for Telara to follow her through the curtained door. "I need to speak with you, without interruptions." She moved through the curtain, not even looking back to see if Telara was following, as if she just assumed that she would. Looking around, she had to admit there weren't many other options for her. Half grunting, half shrugging, she followed.

"No worries, my children," the woman crooned to

a crystal sharded bowl on the wooden table, grabbing a small bottle of crystal dust she poured some shimmering dust into the bowl with two taps of her finger. "I will fix you right up."

"Who are you talking to?" Telara looked around but only saw them in the room.

Low laughter filled the room but no answer was forthcoming. Telara pressed her lips together, swallowing the irritated words that rose in her throat and watched.

The woman picked up a bright silver rod with a sharp looking blade on the end with one while grabbing one of the crystal formations from the shelf above her, the size of a baseball. Clear shards stuck out of a multi-colored crystal sphere the size of a marble. Telara watched as the woman took the silver blade and sliced three slivers off the shards. The slivers fluttered down into the bowl; a sizzling sound could be heard with each sliver. A shimmering cloud rose from the bowl, stifled when the woman placed a green crystal over the top of the crystal bowl. The woman leaned down and blew across the top of the crystal and then said, "Grow for me, baby."

The woman then rose and turned to look at Telara. "Now for you."

Telara took a step back, unsure exactly what that comment meant, considering their daily life they had to worry about shadows literally jumping out at them. "What about me?"

"You're learning more about your powers and how to use them." Her words were spoken in a matter-of-fact manner so Telara felt no reason to respond although her next comment floored her. "About time, I was beginning to think that I was going to have to wait another cycle."

"Uh… sorry." Not sure what she was apologizing about or even why but for some odd reason she felt the need to say it.

The woman gave a slight lift of her right shoulder. "No matter, your powers are starting to show now and that's what matters."

"It is?" Telara wasn't sure if she understood what was going on, none of this made any sense to her.

The woman nodded. "Now we can start."

"We can?" Another nod had Telara frowning. "What are we starting?" she asked in exasperation.

"Why, repairing the realms, of course."

Opening her eyes Telara saw Tia looking down at her with a concerned look. Groaning, she threw her arm over her eyes.

"Did we interrupt something?" her friend asked with a half-smile.

"Just more aggravation." Telara threw back the clovers sliding out of the bed. "I would rather deal with Raven than that woman."

"Wow!" Tia looked over at Vanna who was watching Telara with wide eyes as well.

"Repairing the realms?" Cole repeated as they headed towards the Prime rooms from the cafeteria.

"That's what she said," Telara responded.

"What realms?" Chad asked shouldering between her and Cole who frowned at him.

Telara rolled her eyes. "If I knew that I wouldn't be so aggravated."

"Well, you know, there are more realms out there other than ours," Chad told her, attempting to hold his head high as he strutted along.

"This isn't one of your comic books," Tia told him. "Oomph!" She glared at his back that she had just run into.

Chad turned, giving her an incredulous look. "Did you seriously just say that?"

"Yeah, I did." She crossed her arms, giving him a hard stare.

"You conjure up air, I conjure up ice." He turned towards Telara who was watching the exchange. "Hell, Telly can now conjure illusions and even project them into other's minds." Turning back to Tia he gave a shake of his head, "yet you are denying there could be other realms?"

"What's this about other realms?"

They had been so caught up in their discussion they hadn't even noticed that Zane was coming up on them. Telara turned to tell him about the dream she had when Tia interrupted. "These guys have it in their heads that just because we have powers like their favorite comic book heroes there must be other realms as well."

Telara looked at her quickly.

"Comic book realms huh?" Zane questioned, watching them closely, making Telara feel as if he could see right through them.

"Welcome to a normal daily discussion with the Guardians." Vanna gave a rueful chuckle.

Zane chuckled as he looked them all over, his gaze lingering on Telara who prayed he wouldn't ask her, she wasn't sure she could keep up her friend's ruse and she really didn't like the idea of ousting her friends; even if she didn't agree with them.

"Why don't you guys join me in my office?" Zane

moved away from them, entering the hill ahead of them. They gave each other quick glances before following him. He went down a corridor off to the right then veered to the left until he came to an oversized red wooden door with a set of eyes resembling dragon eyes that seemed to be staring down at them.

Inside they saw a desk that rivaled the desk back in Sanctuary that Lucius had in his office, the same sturdy oak but the decorative legs sculpted to look like dragon legs with large claws that held up the desk. His chair was dark wood with the same claw legs holding up the chair. There were crystal figurines and pieces around the room, and even a crystal bowl that looked vaguely familiar to Telara. Before she could think any more on it, Vanna spoke up, "You must have a thing for dragons."

"What makes you think that?" he asked her.

She gestured around the room to all the architecture that resembled dragon eyes, claws and even the body of a dragon that seemed to wrap around a cabinet. The molding around the top of the wall before it curved into the ceiling was of dragon tails, claws and scales. Along one bookshelf were carvings of dragons climbing up the side by their claws.

Zane chuckled. "You could say that, just like any hunter who displays their trophies."

Telara looked at him, not exactly sure how to respond to that, she could feel Vanna's anger at his words start to pulse inside her and knew she needed to do anything to diffuse the situation before it escalated quickly, Vanna could be the sweetest person you know; until you pissed her off. "When we go back home will we be able to come back; with nothing like the Prime rooms back at Sanctuary, it could be beneficial." Telara ignored the dark looks Vanna threw her way, her lips twitching as she thought about the fact that she was the one trying to diffuse a tense situation. Usually, it was her that was creating the tension, but on the rare occasion that it was Vanna, they did their best to either distract her or intercede in some way.

Zane was now seated in the high back chair behind his desk, his fingers making a steeple as he watched them. "Why?" he asked them simply.

"Not once, since we learned that we were the Guardians, have we ever been able to work our powers like we have in the Prime Rooms," I.Q. spoke up. "I've never completely understood these powers, rather than going on science, I've had to go on faith and trust in a world that I've never believed in. Now, it seems you've given us hope that we could truly defeat the Shadow Master and maybe even come out of this alive. It all rests in those rooms."

"Of course, you can come out of this alive," Zane spoke as if there was no other option. "But you don't need the Prime rooms for that."

"What do you mean?" Chance asked.

"Your powers aren't defined or limited by anything or anyone but you and your own inner insecurities." His words were spoken as if the answer was so simple, as if there was no other answer than that. Yet, they didn't feel the same confidence as he. Their expressions must have given away their thoughts, he chuckled. "You don't believe me."

"It isn't that," Tia said, standing next to the still frowning Vanna, "we just don't understand."

"What isn't there to understand?" He seemed genuinely curious.

"Everything!" The exasperation in Cole's voice was shared with them all as he spoke up, his arms open for effect. "We constantly get told half-truths and yet still expected to go out there to fight a battle we don't understand; a battle that no one expects us to come back from. Now, tell me, is that fair?"

"No, it isn't fair." Zane's face spoke with emotion, emotion that seemed to echo within Telara, it was as if she could feel an echo of pain behind those words, even if she didn't understand it. "Which is why I'm trying to help you, when no one else wants you to succeed, I won't give up until you do."

"So, we can come back here?"

Zane looked over at Telara. "All of you are more than welcome to come back anytime but what I'm trying to tell you is that you don't need to. The power that you've experienced in those rooms aren't because of the Prime Crystals, they are because of you. They're nothing more than an illusion crystal on steroids."

"Yeah, well those crystal steroids have helped us more than any training we've received so far." Chance crossed his arms.

"I'm happy to hear that." Zane's fingers laced together as he moved his head to look at Chance. "That's what they're supposed to be used for. Now, all of you need to take everything you've learned in those rooms and use it outside of those rooms."

"How?" Telara asked him, bringing his gaze back to her.

"Consider that your next lesson." Zane stood up

looking down at his watch that lit up at that precise mo-ment. "But, until then, Billie has requested your presence. I believe she's in the administration offices doing some work with Lucy via crystal vision." He looked back up, his gaze falling on Vanna, who had gone quiet while lis-tening to the conversation. "It seems she wants to show you something."

CHAPTER 15

"Z ane said you wanted to see us." Cole rested his elbows on the counter above the desk where Billie was talking to Lucy on a crystal screen. Cole gave a wink and wave, "how are the Hunters doing? Jeff staying away from your paperwork?" They laughed at the scowl that appeared on her face, even Billie gave a small laugh.

"Have fun Billie, see ya next week?" Lucy gave a wave as they heard Jeff shouting at her from a distance.

Billie turned, the grin still there. "Now that you have my full attention, what can I do for you?"

They stopped and looked at each other then back at her, it was Cole who spoke up, "Like I said, Zane said you wanted to see us."

"Oh, yeah." She hopped up, grabbing her pen on a chain that was lying on the desk next to her. "I have to take a ride out to the borders to check on the crystal barriers." She moved around the desk twirling the chain around her finger heading over to a row of hooks with leather belts hanging from them.

"Crystal barriers?" Chance looked at her; they had never heard of crystal barriers.

"Yeah, the crystals that hide our little haven from the outside world," Billie grabbed a leather belt, attaching it around her waist while clipping on extra crystals. "Was wondering if you guys wanted to go."

They looked at each other. *Any other time I would say yes but I really want to get back to the Prime rooms.* They nodded in agreement, it was Telara who responded to Billie. "Actually, we had something we already had planned."

"Did I mention I was riding unicorns to the border?" Billie moved towards the doorway. "But if you already have plans—" She didn't get her words out when they were all filing in line behind her as she laughed at them, leading them to the stables.

The happiness on Vanna's face as they rode on the unicorns through the trees around the haven, was contagious. The unicorns were such gentle creatures and with the exception of Cole's, none of them gave a hard time about having riders. Billie had to help Cole mount his unicorn as well as give him a hand when the unicorn decided to ignore him and his getty ups, to graze on some grass.

Her fingers moving along the silver mane of the unicorn she was riding, Telara was still in awe of the fact that she was riding on a unicorn. Even though she was able to create illusions with just her thoughts and even levitate herself so that she is able to fly, this had to be the best experience so far.

I concur. She looked over at I.Q. who was trotting along next to her as they moved past the tree line into an open field where the sun glinted off the manes of all the unicorns. She hadn't realized she was thinking her thoughts so loud.

Looking over at Vanna who was very silent, outwardly and mentally although Telara could sense that she was chatting with her unicorn whose mane had a purple hue that glinted in the sun. Telara had tried to have a mental conversation with her unicorn but she wasn't having the luck that Vanna seemed to have. *Could be the fact that Vanna is the reincarnation of Mother Nature.* Tia smiled at her from atop her gray unicorn with a dark mane that had silver highlights.

I can hear you guys, you know that right? Vanna gave them side eyed looks.

Of course, it wouldn't be fun if you couldn't. Vanna gave Chad a dark look at his amused comment.

"And here we are." Billie told them as she dismounted her shiny black unicorn that towered over the rest of theirs. Her Crim was there in her hand as she walked, twirling it around her fingers as she moved.

I like her Crim. Cole chuckled his hand going to his necklace where his finger flicked his red flame crystal. As much as they wanted to laugh at him, they had to agree with him. Following Billie they laughed and shoved each other while their unicorns stayed in the same spot, they left them without even being tethered to anything. Very well behaved.

Of course. Vanna smirked. *Wouldn't expect anything less from such majestic creatures.*

As if you have ridden them before. Chad's sardonic tones shot back. "Hey!" Chad tripped over a clump of grass that they were sure hadn't been there before, he glared up at Vanna who just grinned big not even acknowledging him.

"You know better than to instigate anything with

Savage." Cole chuckled as he helped his best friend off the ground.

"You'd think she would know how to take a joke by now," Chad grumbled, still casting baleful glances Vanna's way.

"You'd think that you would know by now that I always get even," Vanna told him loftily.

"You guys are amusing, my brother should've joined us." Billie shook her head with a smirk as she reached down to grab a crystal they hadn't noticed within the high grass. They looked around them and only saw long grass that had yellowed in the sun, the trees they had passed were so far in the distance they looked like shrubs. Turning back, they watched as Billie twisted her hand around, looking at the crystal from another angle with an intense look of concentration.

"Something wrong?" Telara asked when Billie picked up another crystal that was at least ten feet away, examining in the same manner with the same perplexed expression.

"Not sure..." Billie said slowly looking between the two crystals. "A fully energized border crystal has a slight glow to it but these two have none."

"Are they burnt out?" Chance asked moving closer to Billie.

"If so, then so is this one." I.Q. held up another crystal he picked up off the ground that looked just like the two in Billie's hands.

"Crystals don't burn out." Billie's voice was low as she spoke slowly, staring at the crystals. "I don't understand this."

"What does that mean?" Tia looked around the area.

"It means Haven has no protections." Billie looked up at them. "The better question is how long has Haven been without protection?"

They exchanged looks as the situation they were in started to sink in, looking around I.Q. dropped the crystal in his hand. "Where's Vanna?"

The others started looking around for the absent Vanna, who they swore had been with them only moments before.

"Vanna!"

"Vanna!"

"Van!" They started shouting as they moved out looking for her even though they were in the middle of a grassy field, where could she have gone where they couldn't see her? Clouds above moved across the sky, giving some shade from the hot sun, which might be welcome any other time except shade in their world wasn't always the best sign.

The ground before them erupted as Vanna leapt up, crouching down before them. No dirt, leaves or grass on her anywhere. Her belt gripped tightly in her hand, straightening out on both sides until it turned into her faithful staff as Shadows leapt out after her from the same hole in the ground. "Whoa!" Cole ripped off his necklace as it transformed into his fiery nunchucks.

"Time to go, Guardian!" Chad's ring glowed as his icy sword appeared in his hand, gripping the hilt with one hand while using the other hand to vault over the pile of dirt in front of them, with a sweep of his arm, the sword sliced through the legs of one of the Shadows.

Electrical arrows shot through the air from I.Q.'s bow that formed from his wristwatch, water droplets were felt in the air as Chance's ball and chain appeared from the single diamond earring in his ear while the wind picked up from Tia's arm bracelet that became a crystal whip she used to grab a Shadow's leg. Telara's Rotary started to glow on her wrist, as if it felt the power within her start to burn as she realized what was happening.

"Ambush!" She turned to Billie who was swirling her pen on a chain so fast it started to glow. The glow turned into a blur as Billie moved quickly after a Shadow who dodged Tia's whip. Telara watched as Billie skid through the Shadow's legs, causing the Shadow to let out a screech as the glowing chain wrapped around its leg, Billie gripped the pen and pulled. Telara watched as the Shadow fell to the ground screeching out in pain.

More Shadows erupted from the hole in the ground, taking advantage of the temporary shade the clouds were giving to advance on them. With shade the Shadows were able to camouflage themselves while in the bright sun they were easier to not only see but take down, no shade for them to hide in or use to move through the shadows where they couldn't see them. Looking up into the sky Telara groaned, usually in this Georgian heat the sight of a sky full of clouds was welcome, not while fighting Shadows though.

"Aaaghhh!" A shadow tendril snaked through the grass wrapping itself around Telara's ankle, yanking her down onto the hard ground and pulling her through the grass.

"Telly!"

She heard the shouts from her friends but could see that there were so many Shadows they were unable to get to her as she was being dragged towards several of the shapeshifting Shadows. "Not again!" she shouted as she pulled herself up, staring intently at the Shadows, she thought of the blinding Georgian sun beating down on them. A blinding light that not only hid any escape routes they might come up with but also bright enough to disperse any Shadow brave enough to stand in its way.

The Shadows let out howls that sounded worse than any wounded animal she ever heard of when they saw the light. The tendril that had a hold of her leg went slack, halting her movement. Lifting up her arm with the Rotary she conjured the force shield easier than ever before, bringing her arm down she sliced right through the tendril of the Shadow who let out a wail as the severed tendril slithered back to the ferocious looking Shadow who glared at her. The brightness of her illusion had faded and the Shadows that had cowered from the light were now looking around as if confused.

"Did you do that?" Tia looked over at her in awe.

"Seemed like a good idea at the time," Telara responded.

"It was," Billie shouted. "Can you do it again?"

Telara looked back at the Shadows who were advancing towards her. "Not sure if they will fall for it again, it wasn't real sun, only an illusion."

"Great," Billie grumbled, looking around at the others. "Any other tricks you guys want to pull out of your sleeves?" They looked down at their bare arms. "I didn't mean literally!" Billie gave them an exasperated look as she twirled her pen through the air and let it fly at one of the Shadows who was once again advancing on them. The chain wrapped around the neck of this Shadow, glowing brightly. The Shadow's mouth opened in a soundless scream.

"No!" Grass grew up quickly and pulled off the chain from the neck, which flew back to Billie who was frowning at Vanna as she ran towards the fallen Shadow.

"What are you doing? I was about to destroy the Shadow," Billie protested while the others ran towards Vanna, trying to keep an eye on the other Shadows that were eerily standing around them, not moving.

Vanna knelt by the fallen Shadow, they could see where the chain had been wrapped around its neck was now skin colored. "Could it be?" Telara looked up at Tia and I.Q., who had the same question written on their faces as well. Could this be an Arion that had been changed? They watched as Vanna touched the forehead of the Shadow, her staff in her other hand. Vanna's hand glowed brightly with a green hue, the green hue enveloping the prone Shadow until it dissipated and there on the grass was an unconscious bright red-haired guy.

They looked up at the Shadows around them, the ones that were more humanoid in features backed away, their claws opening and closing as the Shapeshifters moved to the front. "Well, this is different," Chance said, watching them. "No longer wanting to use the minions as fodder."

The shapeshifters seemed to grow more menacing as they moved forward, tentacles flailing and claws extended.

"Line 'em up, " Cole sang out as he twirled his nun-chucks in the air creating heat from the flames that were sparking from not only the nunchucks but also from Cole himself, the Shadows started to move away from him in unison.

"Knock 'em back," Chad sang the second verse as

he swung his icy sword taking out the big gorilla like Shadow closest to him.

"You guys singing Couch Loafers while fighting?" I.Q. let an electric arrow fly that scattered several feline looking Shadows, he turned his head to look at them.

Chad smirked. "What better time?"

"Besides, it fits." Cole slid while his nunchucks were still twirling taking out two lumbering Shadows at the same time.

"They ain't lying," Vanna attempted to get past the wall of Shadows that were blocking them from the minions that were slinking slowly away. "Dang it!" she groused when several Shadows morphed from felines into big bears to stop her.

"Whatcha doing, Van?" Chance asked, swirling his flail around, water droplets falling all around as he wrapped the chain around the leg of a Shadow moose who was rearing up at him. Yanking back there were blood cur-dling screams from the Shapeshifting Shadow in front of him. "Moose belong in Alaska, not Georgia." He grunted.

"You think they care?" His brother snorted.

Chance shrugged, bringing the ball down on the Shadow's head, spraying all of them with water and dis-persing the Shadow in swirling puffs. "Ask me if I care." He looked back over at Vanna who was still attempting to get around the bear.

"I'm trying to get to the minions that are backing away." Vanna's exasperated tone could be felt through them all.

Looking over at the minions, Chance saw that, sure enough, they were moving slowly towards the hole that they had all come out of.

He frowned at her. "Why?"

"Because those ones I know I can heal, the shape shifters just seem to disappear." Vanna moved once more to try to get past the bear who raised its dark paw at her, if not for her quick reflexes of bringing up her staff and blocking it, she could've been knocked out cold.

Telara looked around them. "How do we get Vanna to them before they disappear?"

I.Q. looked around then slowly looked up at the sky above them, his lips quirking at the corners. "Tia, think you can move the clouds out of the way and let the sun shine?"

Tia snorted. "If we were in our rooms, sure, but this is different."

"No, it isn't." Telara got excited looking back to where she had created that illusion, a wide smile breaking free to match the twinkle in her eyes. "It's like Zane told us, the rooms don't truly enhance our powers, they just give us a safe place to learn how to control them." She looked at Tia. "You can do it!" The others joined her with words of encouragement.

Telara's excitement started to become infectious as I.Q. gave Vanna a grin. "Use the earth to get you where you want to be." When Van opened her mouth, possibly to dispute her ability, Cole interrupted her.

"Don't think, just do it!" His eyes glowed with excitement, actually glowing a bright red that seemed to flow through his whole being.

Billie had just taken down a small bobcat shifter with her pen on a chain Crim, turning to Telara she queried, "Think she will be able to do it?"

Telara was still grinning, "damn straight she will."

She looked over at the others. "Let's keep these guys busy and let Tia and Van flex their powers." She looked over at Billie. "Going to join us?"

Billie gave a laugh. "Sure, not like I have anything else planned." She leapt over Cole, landing in a crouched position where she let her crystal pen fly that wrapped around a large python Shadow that was moving towards Tia who was staring up into the sky with concentrated intent.

Electrical arrows flew from I.Q.'s bow as the wind around them all picked up, Telara glanced over at Tia who was rising from the ground, her gaze still on the clouds above them. Tia's arms were outstretched as the wind picked up even more, the tall grass around them waving erratically. Looking up, she saw the clouds starting to move with more speed than normal, shade moving away and sunshine coming out. Tia was doing it.

A blast of cold air startled Telara, turning she saw a frozen statue of one of the shapeshifting Shadows that was in mid-shift from a tiger into something standing on two hind legs, she just wasn't sure what. Looking up just in time she saw Chad leaping in the air and bringing down his sword on the frozen statue. She held up her hands, creating a force shield to deflect the pieces of frozen Shadow that erupted around them.

"Hey!" Chance, who wasn't as lucky as Telara, glared at his brother, who just shrugged with a grin before turning around to go after the Shadow closest to him.

The sun started to shine all around them, effectively taking away all the escape routes for the Shadows who were looking very confused about this change of events. The sound of the ground moving had them looking at where Vanna had been standing but she was no longer there.

"There!" I.Q. was pointing towards where the minions were almost to the hole, there in front of them they saw the earth explode as Vanna jumped out with her glowing staff in hand in the bright sun.

"Whoa!" Billie breathed as she watched. "I'm seeing but having a hard time believing."

Chad ran straight for the shapeshifting Shadows who were growling, hissing and glaring at him. Both hands held out, they watched as ice practically gushed from his hands creating a bridge of ice that went right over the shapeshifters. Chad slid right over them on his bridge, landing behind the minions that were advancing on Vanna. With one swipe of his hand, he blasted their feet with ice, effectively freezing them in place, flailing their arms and letting out garbled shouts.

The air around them crackled, their hair started to stand on end as if they were touching one of those static balls with colored lights. Telara turned to see I.Q. stretching his hand out to the bright sky where storm clouds started to form. The sun! She was about to shout out to him but before she could lightning bolts streaked from the sky down on top of the shapeshifters with flashes of light, blinding them all and disintegrating the Shadows completely.

Their shouts of triumph were short lived as the grass caught on fire, a fire that spread quickly. Chance lifted his hands and brought them down quickly, water coming down in one big wave as if pulled from the air down onto the flames. He looked over at Telara. "There is water in every living thing. I was prepared but I expected that more from Cole than I.Q. honestly."

The laughter that filled the air from that comment was refreshing, it seemed they had won. "Uh… your comment might be premature," Telara said as she looked over at Cole whose body was still glowing, although it seemed to dissipate as he realized that the shapeshifters were gone.

"Nope." Chance gestured to the grass around Cole that wasn't even wilting from the heat. Cole looked at them and grinned.

CHAPTER 16

Those were wicked steps." Billie half walked, half jogged up to them as they stood there. "You guys took care of the Shadows without your Crims. I heard the Guardians were powerful but that was more than expected, better than any superhero movie." The awe shone in her eyes as she looked at them.

"Want to tell your brother that?" Cole asked her, bouncing a fireball in his hand.

Billie arched a brow. "You think he would tell you he was impressed? It takes a lot for Billy to admit he is impressed with anyone."

"Hey!" Vanna shouted at them from over by the hole. "Think you can pause your celebration to give me a hand with these injured Arions?" Turning, they saw several human forms unconscious on the ground by Vanna where the minions had once stood.

"I'll send for med," Billie started to say but Telara gave a shake of her head.

"No need." She turned, looking at the prone bodies on the ground. She didn't let herself think about what she was about to do, she just thought about the forms lifting off the ground and as they watched the bodies seemed to shudder before they rose several inches off the ground.

"My turn." Vanna grinned as the grass around them moved and weaved to create a very large litter of grass twined with some sticks. "Didn't want you to exhaust yourself carrying them by yourself."

Telara laughed. "Much appreciated."

Vanna's eyes lit up with excitement, then with a wave of her hand the hammocks moved across the field until they reached the unicorns where the grass grew and created harnesses that attached to the saddles on the unicorn's back. "We could use you guys at Haven, especially during the games."

"The games?" Chance frowned at her.

"Yeah. They can get intense at times, medical hates them." She laughed. "My brother loves reminding them beforehand just to hear them grouse."

"Vanna earth traveled and then leapt out of the ground right in front of the Shadows!" I.Q. spoke proudly with excitement.

"I froze Shadows! I mean froze them solid!" Chad was holding out his hands and they could feel a coolness in the air.

Telara moved away from him, not wanting to get frostbite. "Tia not only lifted herself off the ground she moved the clouds away from the sun, taking away any escape for the Shadows." Telara looked at Tia who glanced away before smirking. Uh oh.

"Telara created some awe inspiring illusions before she lifted all the fallen from the ground without breaking a sweat." Telara frowned at her but Tia didn't even look her way.

Zane, who had been leaning back in his chair behind his desk, listening to them as they excitedly told him all about their encounter with the Shadows, was now leaning forward, looking at her with a look of pride. "Is that so?"

Telara moved her shoulders nervously in a dismissive manner.

"I'm proud of you all," Zane told them, rising up from his chair.

"I'm ready to go to my fire room." Cole jumped up from his perch on a small bookcase, one that Chance had to reach out and steady quickly before it fell backwards.

Zane threw back his head and let out a bark of laughter. "How about dinner first?" he suggested and everyone laughed when several of their stomachs let out very loud agreements. Seemed battling Shadows was enough to work up an appetite.

❧ ❧ ❧

"So, how do we top that?" Cole watched the performers get things set up on the stage while the techies were adjusting the backgrounds as well as messing with crystals that were situated around the stage.

"Defeating the Shadow Master." Chad looked over at him and suggested. "Coming out of this alive."

"I like that last option." Turning around, they saw Pam standing there on the level right above them.

"Pam!" Cole, Chad, Chance and Vanna jumped up, excited to see her. Telara, Tia and I.Q. didn't move from their seat as they watched Pam, who noticed they didn't give any greeting. She gave a lopsided grin that was very much unlike her.

"I'm sorry guys, I really shouldn't have jumped on you like that," she told them, twisting her fingers.

Telara stayed quiet for a few moments before opening her mouth. "It's all right." She gave a shrug. "We all have our days."

Pam sat down on the bench right behind them.

"Did you figure out what they are hiding?" I.Q. asked her, although the frustration on her face was answer enough.

"They are tight-lipped but I know there is something going on, I just wish I knew who was all in on whatever it is." Pam stared at the stage with an intense expression.

"Hey." Chad leaned forward. "We could always ask Zane, if something is going on in his camp, you would think he would know."

"No!" Pam's sharply spoken word turned several heads around them, until Pam stared at them causing them to look away. She turned back to them and lowered her voice, "I would rather, for right now, we keep this between us." At the frown on their faces she sighed. "I requested another extension, so we have another week, if I don't find out exactly what is going on within that week then we'll talk to Zane and I'll tell him everything I know."

The lights on the stage started flickering, announcing the beginning of the play was about to start, effectively ending their discussion.

The rebels they saw from the earlier shows were on Earth now, living in what must be the first Sanctuary. There were homes in trees and small canvas tents that popped up as well as a large, circus-like canvas tent in the center of Sanctuary. It was in this tent where the rebels were gathered together discussing how they were going to capture the Supreme Ruler, taking her back to their realm and home. It seemed the gods and goddesses of Greece were interfering with their attempts at capturing her.

Looking at each other they felt some fluttering in their guts, this play was starting to feel very familiar. Back on the stage they watched as the rebels mingled with the residents of Greece, making friends and some were even getting closer than that with some. Eight rebels, each with a power that felt very familiar except for one. They weren't sure what her power was, she didn't seem to be doing anything physical but she radiated power. She seemed to be able to affect others around her, they seemed to do what she wanted them to do. She seemed close to the rebel who had freed her from her prison, one whose power was kindred to Telara's. There were two twin females whose appearance had them thinking dark elves from their favorite game, water and electricity were their powers, while a companion to one of the twins sent cold air gusts throughout the crowd. A tall Amazonian woman rode the wind like Tia and another had the gentle attitude they remembered from Mica, not to mention the power Mica and Vanna shared of Mother Earth.

The fluttering in their guts became thousands of butterflies as they watched a very cranky, grumbly, growly beefy male stomped across the stage shooting fire from his palms. They watched as the story of Kull and Safron unfolded before them, the courtship, the wedding, the birth of their twin boys and then the fateful curse. It seemed that no one knew what had happened, just that the town had disappeared from Greece. The rebels raised the twins as they searched for Kull while still attempting to capture the supreme ruler who somehow managed to evade them. Mica left Greece on a lead that was promising a quick end to their search.

More children were born and raised in a Sanctuary that was starting to grow, more mythical creatures running to the rebels for protection from the gods and goddesses that were malicious towards anyone who befriended the rebels or gave them any help at all. And through it all there was the same mysterious male they saw in the Supreme Ruler's palace and the rebel's hideout, still no reason was given for his role in this story. The only distinguishing thing about him was the pocket watch that was always in his hand, the man never spoke during any of the plays, he was just there.

This story is looking familiar but not. I.Q. looked over at them, they gave a very hesitant nod in agreement as they watched the play on the stage, none of this making sense.

Where are the Shadows? Cole voiced the one question that was the loudest in their heads, although their voices felt stuck in their throats as they watched all the scenes unfolding before them. Scenes that were similar but not.

By the time the stage went dark and the actors all took their bows, even the mysterious man, they had all come to the same agreement. They looked at each other but it was Vanna who spoke, "We need to talk to Zane tomorrow." They nodded in agreement as they watched everyone on stage move to clean up. A talk that was overdue.

Telara looked over at Pam but found no recrimination

in her gaze, only the supportive look of her friend. She grinned at her, moving to follow the others to their room and sleep. Sighing she wondered what dream awaited her.

CHAPTER 17

E arthlings are so damn useless."

"Wha—?" Telara looked around, her eyes widening as she realized she was in the back potion room in the house from her dreams. No bed, just the table, shelves with bottles and odd containers full of dust or crystals. There in front of her was the woman with an irritated expression on her face. "What are you going on about?"

The woman turned and looked at her. "About time you got here, we don't have time for dawdling."

"I must be missing something here," Telara spoke but the woman raised a hand to silence her, something that had Telara's lips pressing together to keep the tart words from leaving her mouth, for now.

"We're running out of time and I no longer have the luxury of waiting for you to come to me. Earthlings are so slow."

"Feelings!" Telara's voice rose in indignation as a petite brow rose at her outburst.

"What do feelings have to do with the fact that you're half-human and slow?"

Telara stared at her, momentarily at a loss for words, although that didn't last long. "Half-human?"

The woman sighed. "You're clouding the issue with unimportant facts."

"I disagree." Telara crossed her arms as her irritation rose.

"And you would be wrong."

"How do you figure?" Telara's arms dropped in her astonishment at the gall of the woman before her.

The woman gave a harrumph before responding, "Which do you consider more important? Your precious feelings or the preservation of this barbaric rock you call home?"

"We're trying to stop the Shadow Master, are you offering your help?" Telara couldn't help but wonder if maybe this annoying person could help them defeat the Shadow Master without them losing their lives.

Another arch of that brow told Telara that the woman wasn't offering her help. "He isn't your problem."

"What do you mean he isn't our problem?" Telara was beginning to feel as if she was being punked here, the Shadow Master not their problem? Since when?

"You've been poorly trained and educated. You're just as confused as all the others," was her response.

"Others?"

A dismissive wave had Telara gritting her teeth. "We don't have time for such trivial matters, I only shave a short time to rectify the damage done to the realms."

"Realms?"

A hard stare turned on Telara. "Are you going to repeat everything I say? If you keep interrupting me with these foolish questions, we will never get anywhere. Now do you want to save your world or not?"

Telara was sure that no one had ever aggravated her as much as this woman was doing, and that included Raven, which said a lot. "Well...yeah..." Wasn't that what they had been doing since coming to Sanctuary?

"Very comforting," came the woman's sarcastic retort as she turned away from Telara, moving over to the table with all the jars and bowls of crystals as well as the dust. "Earthlings can be so confusing and it seems you have picked up that bad habit."

"Earthlings confusing?" Telara's voice rose slightly.

The woman nodded as she picked up a round jar with multicolored crystal chips in it, "lazy, argumentative, going to be the cause of their own demise, the list goes on and on." She reached in and pulled out a red chip and dropped it into the crystal sharded bowl on the table.

"No one asked you to come here," Telara told her tightly.

A snort from the table had Telara taking a deep breath. "As if I would sully myself by going to Earth."

"You are on Earth." Telara's voice spoke slowly in her confusion.

"No, we are in my home." Telara watched as she tilted a bottle of blue sparkly dust into the bowl where they heard a hissing sound.

"Which is where?" Telara came back slowly, looking around her.

"Here."

"Ugh! This is aggravating! So, what are you? An alien?" Which honestly shouldn't surprise Telara considering all that she had gone through in the past years.

The woman turned to Telara with a frown. "Alien?

Earthlings have such odd words for that which they can't understand."

"If you're not an alien then what are you?"

"I am the Crystal Keeper," she said as if that explained everything.

"Crystal Keeper?"

The Crystal Keeper gave a long-suffering sigh. "Yes."

"What does that mean?" Telara could see all the crystals across the table and she was fairly certain that colored dust was crystal essence although that was supposed to be volatile even though the woman didn't seem to have any issues with it.

The tone of the woman expressed her impatience at all Telara's questions. "Exactly what it says and as I mentioned, we're running out of time."

"What do you do?"

This time she turned an exasperated look onto Telara that matched the tone of her voice. "I grow the crystals, I tend the crystals, I chose what realm they will thrive in and Earth wasn't one of them."

"Then why are they here?"

The woman's pure porcelain features seemed to glow with anger at Telara's questions, a deep red hue could be seen in her cheeks. "They were brought here by one who sought power they couldn't handle. And now thanks to this person, we need to rectify their damage and take back the crystals, which unfortunately, I need you for."

"But if you take them, how do we defend ourselves from the Shadows?"

"Not my concern, I only care about the crystals."

Telara couldn't believe this conversation. Was this woman for real? The way she spoke about Earthlings, as if Telara shouldn't be offended, and then expected Telara to help her put her world at risk. At this point Telara didn't care about where the woman came from, whether it was another realm or another planet, she was done. "Then I'm not helping!"

The woman's lips thinned as she stared at Telara. "Then I shall just find someone else."

"Fine." Telara grumbled. "Then I'm going back to bed." Crossing her arms, she willed herself to wake up from the dream and within moments she opened her eyes, now staring up at the dirt ceiling above her. She had no idea what to do about that dream, she knew better than to dismiss it but she also wasn't going to deal with it until the morning. Rolling over she closed her eyes sending a silent warning to the crystal woman to leave her sleep alone.

🍂 🍂 🍂

"So, you're half-alien?" The tone in Chad's voice had Telara gritting her teeth, did he have to sound so excited. "Does that mean we're all half-alien?"

"She said she wasn't an alien." Telara gritted out between her teeth. They were walking across the lawn towards Zane's office, she had told them about her dream over breakfast, a breakfast where Pam was once again MIA. She wasn't as upset about that, after their chat last night, they felt a bit more confident. No one even looked at them twice, since this had become their morning routine, although this time their routine was going to be put on hold.

"Crystal keeper," I.Q. murmured softly to himself.

Telara looked over at him. "Have you heard that before?"

"Sounds familiar," he responded slowly as they reached the door to Zane's barracks. "Let's get this over with and then I'll check."

Telara nodded as they reached Zane's office, where the door was indeed open and Zane was moving books around on his bookcase that covered the back wall. He turned looking happy to see them.

"Morning, everything okay with the Prime rooms?"

Telara gave a tentative smile. "They're fine, we just wanted to ask you some questions."

Zane continued moving his books around. "Go for it, as long as you don't mind if I keep reorganizing my books while we chat. Got some new books the other day, so I need to adjust my bookshelf for them."

"Who wrote the play from last night?" Vanna asked from her perch on one of the padded chairs with a wooden back that resembled the back of a dragon, the neck and head created one of the arms while the other arm was a clawed hand. The bottom of the chair was the bottom of the dragon, tail and all.

Zane put away the book in his hand before turning back to look over at her. "I did." Then he grabbed another book that was on a side table close to him.

They looked at each other, they weren't expecting that. Telara turned towards him. "Where did you get the idea or information for the story?"

Zane breathed in deeply, then let it out slowly as he looked down at the books in his hands. Placing them back on the side table he turned around looking at her thoughtfully. "Would you believe me if I told you firsthand?"

Telara took a step back, not sure whether to take him

seriously or not but it was Cole who answered his tone full of sarcasm. "Not unless you were a god or just really, really old."

Zane's head tossed back as he laughed. "Definitely not a god but I am old."

"Not that old," Telara protested.

"Thank you." Zane gave her a wink that seemed to light up his whole face before he continued. "Let's just say that my historians have access to true accounts of the Paladins of old." He moved to sit in his chair behind his desk. "While the other branches of Sanctuary followed Sanctuary's lead and were taught what the gods deemed them taught, I wanted my Arions taught the truth." He reached down into a drawer in his desk and grabbed a book but paused before pulling it completely out. He looked at them with a thoughtful look on his face before opening his mouth. "Can I trust you not to tell anyone at Sanctuary what I'm about to tell you?" They nodded. "Especially Lucius?" His words were very pronounced, as if they meant something more than they seemed.

They frowned and looked at each other, *should we?* Vanna's uncertain question matched the pinched look on her face.

Not like he hasn't held back from us before, Cole's sardonic tone spoke through their mind speak.

Telara snorted in agreement with that remark. *True, and it would be nice to finally have someone tell us everything.*

But will he? Tia looked over at her.

Telara gave a shrug. *Only one way to find out.* Out loud she said to Zane, "I've no problem hiding anything from him, not like he is the model of open communication."

"At least when it comes to us," Chad groused. They nodded in agreement, turning to look at Zane who was wearing a pleased look at their words.

With both hands, he placed the book on the top of his desk, leaning back as he watched the myriad of emotions crossing their faces with an interested look. Almost an exact replica of the book Big Time gave I.Q. back in Alaska. The main difference was the worn etchings in the leather, this book showed the symbols they had always associated with their powers although it wore some new ones as well. A dark puff, a bumpy circle with etchings inside and a circle with swirls as well as jagged lines shooting out joined the symbols they had already known.

He looked up and watched them as they stared at the book, their lips compressed as their looks darted from the book on his desk to the ashen face of I.Q. who had said nothing. "Look familiar?" he asked them.

CHAPTER 18

I.Q. looked over at Telara, who, after a brief hesitation, inclined her head to go for it. Vanna's disapproval could be felt through their connection but they needed answers, answers they weren't getting by keeping their secrets or from the ones who were supposed to be their teachers back at Sanctuary. Vanna's acceptance was grudging but they took it.

I.Q. pulled his book out and showed it to Zane, whose brows raised only slightly, although his lips did curl into a pleased smile. He held out his hand but didn't reach for the book. Looking at I.Q. he asked, "may I?"

There was a brief hesitation before I.Q. leaned forward, placing the book into the palm of his hand. They felt the same apprehension, this was new territory for them all although they knew they needed to try something new. Zane gave an appreciative look before slowly flipping through the pages of the book, as if he was not only seeing the symbols on the pages but reading them as words.

"You understand what is written?" I.Q. asked him.

Zane looked up with a crooked grin. "You could say

after all that I've been through, this is my first language." Before they could ask what he meant, he gestured towards the books on the shelves behind him. "All these books are the true history of not only Sanctuary but the Paladins that you won't find anywhere else. I've translated stories for our historians and players who do the shows at night."

Tia pointed to the book I.Q. had given him. "We were told it talks about the crystals."

Zane looked down. "You were told right. Although this book was long thought to be destroyed, it dates back to even before the Paladins." They gasped in astonishment as they looked at each other and back to Zane who was still looking through the book. "You could say this is a crystal bible. Speaks of someone called the Crystal Keeper who is a crystal Deity."

Telara felt her blood run cold, her words spoken through stiff lips, "Crystal Keeper?"

Zane gave a distracted nod, not noticing the reactions from his offhand comment, still reading through the book with a look of a bookworm devouring their latest treasure.

Maybe he can decipher the Stargazer, Cole looked at them, excitement dancing in his eyes.

Vanna sat up straight in her dragon chair, *I'm putting my foot down on this one, No! You guys don't trust Lucius, well, I don't trust* him!

You're just mad about his dragon remark. Cole looked over at her then ducked behind Chad at her narrowed look.

Enough. Telara frowned at them all, noticing the tendril of one of Zane's plants reaching towards Cole. The tendril slowly started to withdraw at her silently spoken word. *This has to be a unanimous decision, like always. We don't all agree, so we don't show him.* The tendril curled back up in the pot, Telara gave a silent sigh of relief. Vanna wasn't nicknamed Savage for nothing.

Zane looked up. "Do you mind if I keep this? I would, of course, let you know what I translate."

Telara opened her mouth to give permission when Vanna stepped forward. "Would we have permission to check out the ones on your bookshelf?"

Zane gave a shrug of his shoulder. "Sure, anytime, all I ask is that you don't leave my barracks with any of these books."

"We have to read them in here?" Vanna frowned.

Zane laughed. "There is a lounge down the hall that you can use, even a small stocked cafeteria as well. I just ask that they don't go into the Prime rooms, these books are irreplaceable."

🌿 🌿 🌿

"You know, we keep forgetting to ask about that picture." Cole leaned his head down to look down at them as they sat on picnic tables outside the stables where unicorns, pegasi, and the regular horses were neighing out loud. They could hear laughter from the pond as well as sounds of splashing. They looked at each other, realizing the truth in Cole's words, then groaned.

"Seriously?" Chad fell back on the top of the wooden table. "The main reason we have come here and we fail every time when we really need to ask the person who probably knows everything about our past Guardians."

"Not like we haven't had other things to distract us."

Vanna pointed out. "Getting to learn our powers as we have, the plays once thought of as fiction that could now be the history of our ancestors."

"Yeah." I.Q. straightened up from his perch on a wooden bench of the table.

Cole looked over at I.Q. whose expression seemed to light up. "What's up, I.Q. man?"

"If those stories are the history of the past Guardians, you realize that the original ones came from another world," I.Q. told them.

"What do you mean?" Tia leaned forward, the others waited to hear his response.

"The play about the rebels uprising to take down the female Supreme Ruler, they went through a portal like opening," I.Q. reminded them. "That was them escaping their world and coming to ours."

"Hey, that's right!" Chad exclaimed, then pointed to Telara. "That lady said you were an alien, that must mean we're all aliens!"

Chad and even I.Q. seemed to look excited but everyone else had gone pale at the prospect.

"We don't know that for sure," Vanna told him, a brow lifted when he opened his mouth to say something, he closed his mouth quickly and just looked down at the ground in front of him.

"It doesn't matter if we're descended from aliens or Gods, not if we end up dying in the end." Chance's words sobered them up.

"It does if it keeps us from suffering the same fate as the Guardians before us," his brother spoke up.

They looked at each other but it was Telara who spoke, "So in other words, knowing about the past

Guardians could or could not help us. Mastering our powers could or could not help us. Deciphering the Stargazer could or could not help us. Translating the crystal book could or could not help us." She was ticking each item off with her fingers, she looked up from her fingers. "In other words, we know NOTHING for certain," her voice started to break. Tia moved to comfort her but Telara brushed her off, standing up and walking away. "I just need some time."

The others watched her walk away from them, feeling hopeless to help their friend.

Telara heard the others come into the outside room that made up the main living area of their rooms, their low murmuring as they tried not to disturb her as she lay under her covers in her bed. She stayed still and silent as Tia and Van moved into their sleeping quarters, pretending to be asleep so she didn't have to answer any questions.

As she lay there, she let her mind wander trying to stave off this feeling of hopelessness that was doing its best to engulf her. No matter what they did, they never seemed to get closer to the answer of how to survive, if there is an answer. Unlike the stories and movies they have read or watched, there was no prophecy to tell them what to do. All they got was songs and that rhyme of Soleil's.

Her eyes popped open and it took all her willpower not to sit upright in her bed as a realization dawned upon her. The last line of that rhyme was the seven will bring forth heaven or something like that. What if she said Haven instead of heaven and they just thought it was heaven? Could this place be the answer they have been looking for? Closing her eyes, she willed herself to relax and sleep, maybe talk with her friends about that tomorrow. Maybe they did get a prophecy after all.

"About time you showed up," the voice of the woman from her dreams interrupted her thoughts. When she opened her eyes, she was once again in the home of the mysterious woman who watched her with a touch of irritation in her expression.

Telara looked around her; they weren't in the bedroom she woke up in the beginning nor were they in the potion type room with all the bottles. This room had portraits all along the wall to her right that looked as if they were different scenes, one looked like the streets of New Orleans, another had people of all different colors walking along cobbled streets and yet another looked as if it was an underwater world with blueish green people swimming around.

Telara moved closer to the pictures, reaching out for a picture with some figures walking through streets in a rural setting. Lights that resembled crystals adorned posts along the walkway, they were dressed in purple robes with crystal adornments. She looked back at the lady who was watching her. "Where is this?"

"What does it matter?" Her purplish brow furrowed at Telara.

"Nothing, so why not tell me?" Telara countered.

"It's a realm far away from this one." She gave a dismissive gesture of her hand, her expression showing disdain for even having to answer the question.

"Realm?" Telara's eyes widened as she looked at all the pictures. "Are these all realms?"

"Yes." The woman huffed in annoyance. "But they don't matter."

"Don't matter?" Telara looked at her then back to the pictures. "I would think the ones who live within them would disagree." Even as she said that she marveled at how easily she took what the woman said for fact. She was talking to a woman who has only shown up in her dreams, looking into pictures of other realms and not having a nervous breakdown. Years ago, she would have thought she had gone crazy but now? Now, it's just another day in the life of being a Guardian. "Thought you needed me to help repair the realms, these realms right?"

"You're wasting time on trivial matters." A hand waved in a dismissive gesture, a gesture Telara had seen too many times since meeting this woman.

"These may be trivial to you but this is all new to me." The woman frowned at the exasperation in her tone. "Look," Telara started to say then paused, "what do I call you?" She had just realized that not once during their encounters has the woman introduced herself.

"What?"

"Your name," Telara responded. "I don't know what to call you."

"What does that matter? Why must you ask such trivial questions?" The woman's purple brow furrowed.

"Because these trivial questions aren't trivial to me!" Telara's voice rose in her agitation.

The woman gave a long-suffering sigh. "Kyler, my name is Kyler. Now are you happy?"

"Kyler," Telara spoke the name slowly, trying it out on her tongue, then she grinned at Kyler. "I like it."

"I don't care." Kyler moved past her and the pictures of the realms adorning one of the walls in this room.

Telara turned around with a frown, her mouth opening to respond to Kyler's rude comment but whatever words she was about to say stuck in her throat as she looked at the wall Kyler was standing in front of. In the middle of the slatted wooden wall was a swirling circular mass of purples, silvers and blackness that weaved all around each other, covering most of the wall in front of them.

"What is that?" Telara moved slowly closer to the wall, reaching out to touch the wall but jerking her hand back quickly, holding it to her protectively.

"It won't hurt you." Kyler's droll voice matched her eye roll. "This is taking too long."

"What is?" Telara looked back at Kyler, who was now standing behind her.

"You." Kyler stared at her. "It's time for you to find out who you truly are."

"Wha—" Telara started to ask her but broke off in a shriek when Kyler shoved her into the swirling colors on the wall. ""Aahhh!"

CHAPTER 19

"Hey T!"

Telara looked around her, not sure exactly where she was but it wasn't in Kyler's place nor was it back in Haven. She was outside but there were no barracks in any hillside with wooden doors and no coliseum in the center. A great tree that was reminiscent of the Elder tree back at Sanctuary stood behind her although this tree had a double door that was big enough for a giant to walk through. There were several smaller trees around with doors the size of small houses as well as some huts that were built from sticks and leaves. Behind wooden fences were lambs, goats and even some pigs.

She thought Kyler's looked like it was created right out of a fairytale, this place was even more so. Cobbled walkways connected the houses while dirt roads could be seen in the distance. This was a town, one that was touched by magic. Just as she thought that, she saw a gnome leave one of the smaller thatched huts outside one of the fenced in yards with pigs, his stubby fingers gripping the rope of a wooden bucket he was carrying. The gnome ambled over to a trough on the other side of the fence, he clumsily lifted the bucket and poured the slop into the trough.

"T!"

Telara let out a surprised yelp when a pair of masculine hands gripped her shoulders. She let out a sigh of relief when she saw Cole grinning down at her. "Giant!" She griped, pushing at him.

"Giant? Where?" Cole looked around, worried.

Telara rolled her eyes. "Don't be such a dork."

"Dork? What is a dork?" Cole looked back at her; it was then that she noticed the clothing he was wearing. The same clothing they saw the actors on the coliseum stage wearing during their plays about the Paladins in ancient Greece.

"Why are you wearing those?" She frowned at his clothing, ignoring his question.

"Tien, are you okay?" Cole peered down at her, his face full of concern.

"What did you just call me?" She looked up at him feeling as confused when she had during any of her talks with Kyler.

"Tien! Zeke!"

Telara gasped, there was Zach running towards them with an excited gleam in his eyes. When he reached them, he put his arm around her waist, kissing her head as he looked at Cole.

"Really, brother?" Cole gave him an affronted look. Telara looked between the two, not sure if she was sure what she was hearing. Did Cole just call Zach his brother? What was going on here?

Zach laughed, giving Telara a squeeze as he looked down at her. "Your mother is back and asking for you."

"My mother?" Telara asked slowly, looking between the two.

"Yeah, your mother,. Zach laughed. "You know, the leader of Sanctuary and not someone who likes to be kept waiting. Let's go before she skins us for keeping you."

"Sure," she responded weakly, letting Zach lead her away from the tree houses down the dirt road. As they walked, she looked around them, their words as they talked and clowned around with each other wafting around her, the fact that she was silently looking around her in bewilderment seeming to escape their attention. She noticed crystal clusters sprouting up in grassy clusters that were being tended by small fairies. A gnome lumbered with a wooden bucket along the road, reaching down and pulling up a few colorful crystals before tossing them into the bucket with a thunk.

Not only did she see the magical creatures around them but there were also people working alongside them. A woman in a cotton dress was pulling up a bucket of water from a stone well and pouring it into one of the buckets a centaur was carrying. Little boys ran around in cotton pants and shirts while a little girl scrambled to keep up with them in her little blue dress with a dingy white apron tied around her waist. She felt the air leave her lungs when she saw small canvas huts, the same canvas huts that were in the play from last night.

Where was this place Kyler sent her? Zach was calling Cole 'Zeke', and they were acting as if they were brothers. They were calling her 'Tien' and taking her to see someone they said was her mother. She was trying to piece this together but she felt as if she was adding two and two together only to come up with five. She came to a sudden stop, there in front of them was the large circus-like tent from the play as well. Sanctuary, this was the original Sanctuary. But how?

"Tien!" A woman with flowing blond hair came bursting from the tent with a smile, embracing Telara as both Zach and Cole/Zeke moved out of the way. "I've so missed you while we were away." Was this the same blond rebel leader from the play?

She wasn't sure what to say so she just gave a small nod as the woman hugged her, something the woman noticed, her brow furrowed slightly as she looked down at her, "something wrong?" Not trusting herself to speak, Telara just gave a small smile and shook her head. The woman laughed and pulled Telara into the circus tent, "come inside and tell me what you've been doing while we were away. We really didn't expect to be gone so long and we missed you so much." She let herself be pulled into the tent, her eyes going wide when she saw the paintings on the heavy canvas walls. Serdita played her Chenras and even Soleil with her silver fiddle.

"Marsella." Telara turned away from the paintings as a male, whose skin glowed a light blue hue, entered along with two women who were almost identical. They were the same height, same build, both had skin dark as night and silver hair with purple and blue hues. The only difference between the two was the color of their eyes. One of them had brilliant blue eyes while the other twin's eyes were deep purple with silver flecks. The male pushed back his long pearl-white hair with both hands, then let his hands fall to his sides which released his hair to fall around his face before settling back in feathered waves. He had a roguish grin on his sculpted face while his dark eyes twinkled. They were from the play as well, water and electricity. The male had the power of ice.

"Plax! Kala! Kali!" Marsella turned from her and rushed to hug them. "Please tell me that you have news."

Her smile slipped at the look on his face. "I'm sorry Mars, we can't find any sign of any of them."

Marsella's back straightened as she fixed her smile back on her face. "I refuse to give up, we will find them."

"That's the spirit!" The male hugged Marsella to him before turning to the twin with blue eyes. "Kala, my love, would you fetch our boys and the other children?"

She nodded before leaning up on tippy toes and kissing his lips. Sharply turning on her heel she practically glided out of the tent. A cool breeze wafted out behind her.

The air filled with the fragrance of a bouquet of flowers as the flaps of the tent moved apart with the help of green vines and in sauntered Vanna, although this time Telara pressed her lips together before she said something wrong like calling this person Vanna. "Any news of my mother?" Her green eyes looked at Plax and Kali.

"I'm sorry, Jacinta," Kali reached out for her but Vanna/Jacinta flinched away. "Nothing of your mother, Kull, Safron, or Zo."

Vanna/Jacinta looked down at the ground where the vines that were already drooping in sorrow with their mistress, lay. A single tear rolled down her cheek, over the bridge of her nose until it dropped onto the hard ground below. Telara twitched as she fought the urge to go to her friend and hug her, she wasn't sure if whoever she was playing right now was friends with Vanna/Jacinta.

"Papa!" In walked Chad and Chance with I.Q. and Tia following closely into the large tent.

Plax turned and clasped both Chad and Chance on their shoulders. "Axel, Egon. Have you two been behaving yourselves while me and your mother have been gone?"

Cole/Zeke and Zach coughed when the two brothers attempted to speak up and declare their good behavior. Their coughs silenced when Plax raised an eyebrow at them, turning back to his sons. His smile wavered as he looked at Tia who watched him silently. "Ah, Chantria, I'm sorry, we couldn't find any information of your father."

Tia/Chantria pressed her lips together as she attempted to smile. "My father is too stubborn for any old witch to best him. We'll find him." Plax put his arm around her and gave her a gentle squeeze.

"That's the girl." She smiled and moved out of his embrace to stand next to I.Q. who was silently watching all.

"You know Tien," Kali moved closer to Telara, speaking softly, "I don't think I have ever seen you this quiet, is everything okay?"

Telara shook her head realizing everyone's attention had turned towards her, not something she wanted to happen. "Everything is fine, nothing wrong with me." Besides the fact that she was apparently in someone else's body talking with people who look like her friends but weren't and let's not forget the others who seemed to be the Paladins from the plays at Haven.

Kali gave a thoughtful look. "The other option is that you're up to something."

Telara blanched, her eyes going wide as she stared back at Kali, trying to think of what to say to appease her. Kali grinned as she gripped Telara's shoulder and gave a gentle squeeze. "Just keep your mischief inside Sanctuary, the Gods and Goddesses out there aren't very happy with us and will use any means they can to hurt us."

Telara nodded. "That I can do."

"Good." Kali lay her cheek on the top of Telara's head as she squeezed gently before moving away to where I.Q. watched. "Dell, have a hug for your mother?" I.Q. moved to hug the woman as Telara watched, feeling as if she was starring in a movie she had never seen.

Marsella's golden blond hair shimmered with each movement as she stood around the large oval wooden table that seemed to dominate the portion of the tent they were standing in. Kala and Plax were on the other side of the table, their fingers intertwined as they spoke with Marsella and Kali. Marsella looked down at the table, her brow furrowed in concentration. The top of the table was glowing with images reminiscent of a gaming screen like ones back home in the game rooms. Although she was sure this didn't work with a few quarters, nor did she believe that the images flashing about were fictional.

The tent was sectioned by heavy drapes that hung from the ceiling, the room they were in seemed to be the biggest and the main one, with smaller rooms sectioned off towards the opposite side of the tent. There were nymphs walking around, fairies flying through the air and mermaids in small pools dug into the ground. So, this was the original Sanctuary; she wasn't sure if this was freaky or really cool.

"I hate agreeing with our parents but you really are being too quiet, Tien." She looked over at Tia/Chantria who had moved to stand next to her, looking at her with suspicion. She hoped this meant that they were as close back then as they are now.

Telara gave a slight shrug of her shoulders. "Just wanting to hear what the adults are talking about."

"What they're always talking about." Zach joined them with Zeke, he grinned at Telara and she felt a flutter in her stomach at that smile.

"And what's that?" she asked, in her curiosity, forgetting that she was staying quiet so as not to raise suspicions.

"Finding the missing members of our family," I.Q./ Dell said, watching her suspiciously. "Zo, Mica, Kull and Safron. Finding them and bringing them home."

"Don't forget taking out Lara while we're at it so we can truly go home," Chad/Axel said with a cold grin. "Time for her to pay for her crimes."

"Let's join them and see what they found out." Cole/ Zeke gestured towards the table where the adults were all talking.

"As if they would even tell us." Telara couldn't stop the snarky comment from slipping through her lips.

"Of course they would," Vanna/Jacinta told her. "Why would you say something like that Tien? Haven't they always been honest with us? Even when it was something as painful as the disappearance of Zeke and Zach's parents?" Her voice held censure but her eyes looked at her with a wary expression. She was truly messing this up, but she didn't know where she was, who she was supposed to be or even worse, how she should be acting.

Tia/Chantria turned Telara around and pointed to the paintings that adorned the fabric walls of the tent behind them. "We're the children of the Paladins, the protectors of the innocent and friends to all. We help our parents in their quest to heal the crystals and stop Lara from taking the true power of the crystals for her own. In the event of their demise, it is our responsibility to carry on their quest and once the crystals are reunited, we get to finally see our true home. Have you forgotten?"

Telara stared at the pictures beautifully painted on the heavy fabric, there in front of her was the picture that they had seen in the Stargazer as well as a picture of each of her friends that were standing next to her now. Underneath each picture was their name so elegantly drawn. She turned, seeing more drawings, there was Kull with his ever-present scowl and a smiling Safron at his side. Before she could look through all the Paladins portraits as well a voice had her frozen in place.

"How went the hunt?" She turned to see Lucius standing there with a grin on his face looking from the Paladins over to them, and when his gaze lit upon hers, he actually winked. Her stomach felt as if it crash landed on the ground.

CHAPTER 20

Lucius." Marsella gave a welcoming grin. "Welcome home."

He looked at her with a smile then looked over at the rest of them. "Any sign of the others?"

Plax shook his head. "No sign of any of them, it's as if they vanished into thin air."

Lucius gave a sad sigh, pulling a pocket watch from his pocket. Telara stared at the watch, the mysterious man from the play, the one who had stood on both sides. What was going on? Nothing was feeling right, it was as if she had just been tossed into the middle of the ocean with no raft, boat or life jacket. Snapping the watch closed and sliding it into his pocket he let out an aggravated breath. "We need answers."

Telara looked at Lucius, not understanding why he was acting as if he knew nothing. "It was the Gods, you know that. Why are you acting as if you don't know?" Telara couldn't stop her outburst.

"Tien!" Marsella's voice rebuked her hastily spoken words. "You know we can't make accusations without any proof."

Plax snorted. "You sure she isn't related to Kull in some way?" He held up his hand when Zach frowned up at him. "That wasn't meant in a disparaging way, I miss your father as well but usually the hot-tempered outbursts are his style."

Zach seemed to settle back next to Telara giving a half shrug. "Not that I have any memory of my father but that is the consensus on him from what I've heard."

"Your father is a good man, just one with a short fuse." Lucius chuckled.

"One you have been known to set off a time or two," Plax told him with a grin, to which Lucius just smirked.

"Sometimes, you have to find your entertainment where you can."

Marsella rolled her eyes. "And sometimes you can take it too far." Then her stern gaze turned onto Telara. "And you will show your grandfather respect when you speak to him or you will find yourself in your room with no company for a spell."

Telara pressed her lips together and looked down, hoping no one saw the shock in her face. Lucius, her grandfather? How? When the conversation still didn't resume after a few moments she looked up to see Marsella still looking at her, that was when she realized that she was waiting for an answer. She wasn't sure how the person whose body she was residing in would respond but hoped she had it right when she nodded, "yes, mother." Must have been close enough when after a slight hesitation Marsella gave an approving grin before turning her gaze back to the images on the table before them.

"Anything new from Serdita or her siblings?" Plax asked Lucius.

"Just that all is happening as foretold." Lucius sounded aggravated, something that did give Telara some tiny bit of satisfaction. "Getting a complete answer from any of them is harder than the stones on Mount Olympus."

"Sometimes Kull has it right, Melonians can be a complete pain." Plax grimaced then looked over at Marsella quickly. "Sorry Mars."

She held up a dismissive hand, "no apology needed. My people can be aggravating and very much stuck in their ways. They believe because they see things others can't, that it makes them all-knowing."

Cole/Zeke snorted. "All-aggravating maybe." Telara expected him to be reprimanded but instead the others laughed in agreement. The fact that they were discussing everything in front of them and even letting them join in on the conversation had her wishing this was her reality. Cole/Zeke sobered. "The prophecy says we win right?"

Kala looked at Lucius, who wore a grimace. "You know how prophecies go, vague and easily changed." Lucius looked down at the images moving around on the table in front of them.

"Have you been able to get the prophecy from Serdita?" Kali asked him.

Lucius snorted. "Have you ever tried getting something from her that she didn't want to give?"

"But the prophecy is about all of us," Vanna/Jacinta protested. "Doesn't she want us to win, this affects her and her family as well."

Lucius gave a wry grin. "She knows this but it isn't her way."

"Her way is going to get us killed." Zach leaned on

the table, staring down at the images, his expression hard to read.

"Let's hope not." Marsella placed a comforting hand on top of his.

"As soon as Lara entered this realm, she changed the original prophecy that brought her here, according to Serdita," Lucius grumbled.

"Are we sure we can trust her?" I.Q./Dell asked him.

"When it comes to Serdita there is no assurance either way, but to ignore her could be just as disastrous as listening to her." Telara could hear the frustration in his voice as Lucius spoke, she tried to not feel bad for him but she couldn't help it.

Plax gave Lucius a droll look. "Lucius, I swear you are part Melonian. Probably why you and Kull are always at odds." There were several snickers around the table at that remark.

"Serdita feels that giving away too much of the prophecy could endanger the outcome needed to stop Lara from her plans." There were several grumblings about the validation of Serdita's words.

Telara looked up at Lucius to ask about the Shadows but before she could, the world around her started to swirl around as a hand grabbed her shoulder. She turned around and she was back in the room with Kyler. "What was that?"

"That was your past life," Kyler told her. "Your past life, who failed in her duty, now her duty falls to you."

"Who is Lyra?"

"A traitor who hasn't been brought to justice." Kyler watched her as she seemed to grapple with what she saw.

"What of the Shadow Master?" Telara asked. "They

didn't bring him up once, it was all about Lyra and finding those who went missing."

"I told you the Shadow Master didn't matter." Kyler rolled her eyes.

"Just because they didn't mention him or the Shadows, doesn't mean he doesn't matter when he threatens my world and loved ones." Telara crossed her arms. "You said you would help with the Shadow Master, that little trip changes nothing."

The woman scoffed. "I can't believe that you are the one in the prophecy, so many inane worries."

Telara crossed her arms. "Sucks to be you, I guess."

"We'll talk more later." Kyler walked away from her.

"Does that make us reincarnations?" Tia had a small tornado dancing in the palm of her hand. They were sitting by the pond watching mermaids play around in the water with some of the Arions.

Telara pulled the tornado to her hand but it fizzled out when it touched her skin, and they laughed. She sighed staring at her hand. "Seems that way."

"Children of the Paladins." I.Q. looked down at his closed Stargazer.

"What is it?" Vanna looked over at I.Q. who was tapping the cover of the Stargazer.

"Not sure but sure seems like Kyler was right." Telara looked sharply up at him, he looked back at her. "This is about more than just the Shadow Master."

"Sounds to me as if everything we were told is nothing but lies." Cole leaned back on the grass looking up at the sky above them. "Seems like Lucius and several others have some explaining to do."

"That he does." Tia looked over at Telara. "He really called you his granddaughter in the vision."

Telara shrugged. "Marsella did."

"Hey there." Billie plopped down next to them on the ground along with another cute little Arion with purple pigtails, both of them pulling out their phones and scrolling through videos.

Telara looked over at them with a furrowed brow. "Uh … hi." Then looked back at the others who were watching Billie.

"Whatcha watching?" Cole looked over at her.

"Some Jak-Jak videos." Billie scrolled up on her phone. "Logan was telling me about a new trend they were starting on there about walking in Alligator pits."

"You're kidding?" Chad moved quickly to her side, looking over her shoulder. "You guys actually use social media?"

Billie looked back at him with a deadpan stare that had him backing away, looking chagrined. "What do you think we are? Neanderthals?" He opened his mouth to apologize but she wasn't done. "You know, the technology we have here beats anything you will find on your world wide web."

"Uh, sorry," he stammered but she had already turned away, watching the next video. The others snickered as Chad looked lost and unsure what to do.

Cole looked from the girl to Billie before asking Billie, "Plan on introducing us to your new little friend?"

Billie snorted. "If she wants you to know her name, she can tell ya."

Purple pigtails giggled and Cole grumbled about her sounding just like her brother. Purple pigtails held out her hand. "The name is Aundrea."

Cole took her hand and held it, staring at her. "Aundrea. Nice name."

Aundrea looked down at their hands then back up at him. "Thanks, I like it too." Then she looked back down at their hands that were still intertwined in greeting. "Can I have my hand back?"

Cole looked down as if just realizing he hadn't let go of her hand. "Sorry, uh, yeah." He let go of her hand quickly.

"Thanks." She moved back to her phone.

Cole pulled out his phone from his pocket, looking from his phone back to her, she looked up from the phone as she felt his eyes on her. Cole cleared his throat. "Ummm… I seem to have lost my number, can I have yours?"

The silence around them was deafening as the Guardians looked from Cole to Tia who was glaring at him. The others were looking rather nervous as they waited for Tia to send Cole flying into the pond. Aundrea just smiled, pulling out a piece of paper and writing on it before she stood up and handed the folded paper to Cole, "Sure." With that she turned and walked away.

Uh-oh. I.Q. looked nervously at Tia who was watching Cole unfold the paper.

"What the?" Cole frowned.

"What's up?" Chad reached for the paper but Cole quickly moved to keep it from his grasp.

"Nothing, go away." Cole glared at him. "Hey!" He turned and tried to grab the paper but it was too late, Billy looked down at the piece of paper he swiftly snatched from Cole.

"1-800-not on your life." Billy chuckled. "Dude, you

just got flat tired." He tossed the scrap of paper back at Cole who had gone from glaring to frowning.

"Flat tired?" Cole frowned at Billy.

"Yeah," Billy told him. "Means she just let the air out of your tires." He walked away chuckling.

"Flat tired," Tia mused with a grin. "I like it."

"You would," Cole grumbled.

CHAPTER 21

Telara watched the Arions of Haven working out on the training field, the others were in their Prime rooms playing around. So much had happened since they came to Haven, even more than they have been through in the past several years since coming to Sanctuary. Leaning against a lone tree outside the training area, the rough bark biting into her soft skin, Telara gave a small sigh.

"Out here all by yourself?" Telara turned around to see Zane standing there watching her. "Figured you would be with your friends playing in your room with your powers."

She gave a shrug and let out a long sigh. "Just seem to have a lot on my mind lately, tired of being lied to, tired of not knowing what's going on."

"That's understandable." He nodded, moving forward to stand next to her, watching the training. "I try to make it a practice to always tell the truth when possible. You can't ask for trust if you aren't willing to give it."

Telara snorted, "You need to teach Lucius that."

Zane scoffed softly. "Some lessons can't be taught."

He turned to her. "I can't control what Lucius does or doesn't do, only myself. Would you like to join me in my office? I was about to make some tea and I find myself wishing for company. Unless you would rather be by yourself," he hastened to add when she seemed to pause.

She looked back at the training field, "I think I've spent enough time by myself." She turned to him. "I could do with some company as well."

Zane smiled and gestured for her to take the lead to his office, after a brief hesitation she started forward, head held high.

"Raspberry chocolates?" Telara closed her eyes as the bitter sweet candies melted in her mouth, as soon as she entered his office she saw the bowl of chocolates and couldn't resist taking one, after she asked permission, of course. "I love these. The best combination ever made."

Zane chuckled. "I couldn't agree more. You go ahead and enjoy the chocolates while I go and grab the tea, will be right back."

Telara gave an absent-minded nod as she reached for another one of the chocolates, not even paying attention to him as he left. So much was on her mind, that for once she enjoyed the fact of being a teenager eating sugary sweets and not listening to an adult lecture her on what was expected of her. Growing up, they read fantasy stories about teenagers with powers or some other special abilities that they used to bring down the villain of the story. They always fantasized about being the hero in the stories, they were idiots.

She walked around the office, her fingers running

over the surface of the desk, bookshelves with the dragons climbing upwards and even the side tables in the room. Picking up knickknacks and examining them. There were pictures lining the bookshelves of people she knew and some she didn't. There were the crystal pieces scattered along the top of a nearby coffee table, one piece was the small bowl with crystal shards making up the outside of the bowl. Picking up the bowl she admired the blues, greens and golds woven within the crystals.

"That's a Kurn." Turning around, she saw Zane standing there with a tray of hot water, cups and tea bags. He placed them on the table with all the crystal pieces.

"A Kurn?" Telara turned over the bowl in her hands, wasn't that big of a bowl, looked more like a trinket holder. "What's it used for?"

Zane shrugged as he poured them both some hot water into their glasses. "Don't know, it's just a family trinket that has been handed down from generation to generation." He handed her a cup and then sat down. "If you listen to my grandmother, it was used to create new crystals but to me it's just a small bowl."

"Create new crystals?" Telara looked from the bowl to him, then back to the bowl. She was sure she had seen a bowl just like this. "How would a bowl do that?"

"Magic." Zane grinned at her. "You can't say you don't believe in magic." He snorted at the look of disbelief on her face. "The person who can fly with just her mind."

"Levitate," she corrected him. Then laughed at herself when he raised a brow at her words.

"Changing the word doesn't change the facts." Zane informed her.

"There you are." She looked up to see the others entering Zane's office looking tired but also pleased with themselves. Cole continued, "We looked in your Prime room but you weren't there."

She gave a small shrug. "Wasn't in the mood to play with powers, went for a walk and then Zane found me."

"Lunch!" Cole's eyes lit upon the chocolates and sandwiches on the tray on the table, he moved forward until a gust of wind pushed him back. He glared back at Tia who shook her head trying to hide her amusement. "What? I'm hungry! Practicing powers works up an appetite."

"Where are your manners?" Tia reprimanded him. "You weren't invited."

Cole frowned at her then gave the food on the table a sorrowful look, Zane threw back his head letting out barks of laughter. "Please, join us, there is plenty of food for all." He shook his head with amusement when Cole, Chad and even Chance bum rushed the table.

"Never get in the way of these guys and food," I.Q. told him with a smirk as he watched them.

Zane turned to look at I.Q.. "I've been reading the book you loaned me."

I.Q. looked at him with interest. "Really?" All eyes were on Zane, well except the three boys who were still piling food on their plates. Telara wondered if Zane knew they would be having guests since there was a small pile of plates on the tray, she hadn't noticed that earlier.

"Yeah, it's real interesting reading," Zane replied.

The boys sat back with their plates while the others moved to grab some food now that it was safe. When everyone was seated with a plate, Zane continued, "It reads almost like a history book all about the crystals, though it does mention Crystal Lords, Keepers and Seers."

Telara gasped when he said Keepers, bringing his attention right to her while the others bit their lips and watched her. "Something sound familiar?"

Opening her mouth, she paused and slowly closed her mouth, unsure about telling him everything. Pam's warnings in the back of her mind had her hesitating, but she hated the thought of hiding something from the only one who seemed to be honest and truthful with them. Licking her lips, she tried to pick her words carefully. "Just something I dreamt about." She wasn't lying, she told herself and felt the supporting glances from her friends.

Zane watched her thoughtfully. "You know, there are some who say that dreams are your past lives speaking to you."

Telara gave a wry chuckle. "I think mine are screaming at me."

"Maybe they are attempting to warn you about something," Zane suggested. "It could do you well to listen to them."

Telara nodded, looking down at her hands unsure of how to respond. I.Q. thankfully turned the attention away from her when he pulled out the Stargazer from his pocket, attracting Zane's attention and surprisingly getting no argument from Vanna who was sipping on her tea as she watched silently. "Think you could understand this?"

Zane reached for the Stargazer, they watched as the Stargazer transformed from the small disk in his hand to the small laptop, there on the screen was the picture of

Telara that had brought them here. Zane looked up at her.

"That's kind of what brought us here," she admitted slowly.

"I was looking up any information I could on the Paladins and any of the past Guardians when that picture came up, looks just like her except for the ancient type clothing she wore." I.Q. watched him as he explained.

"And the fact that I know that isn't me," Telara supplied.

"Are you sure about that?" Zane asked her.

Telara snorted. "I'm pretty sure I would remember a picture like that being taken of me."

Zane shrugged, tapping the keys as if he was typing on a regular laptop with even more confidence than I.Q. had with it. They watched as the name Tien appeared under the picture, they looked at each other, butterflies coming to life in all their stomachs.

"That's what brought us here," I.Q. reiterated what Telara had said earlier. "Why does she look exactly like Telara?"

Zane looked over at Telara, his eyes shining brightly, bringing a lump to her throat that she couldn't understand. Looking back at the picture he gave a small sound in his throat. "Could the prophecy have come to pass after all?"

"Prophecy?" Tia tilted her head.

He seemed lost but at the sound of Vanna clearing her throat, he looked up. "There is a prophecy that the children of the Paladins will reunite to right an old wrong and restore the power of the crystals. With their children, the Paladins would once again walk among us."

"Restore the power of the crystals?" Chance was leaning back against the desk, his right hand moving to his ear where his Crim was nestled on his lobe as the crystal earring. "They seemed to be working fine to me."

"The crystals weren't created to battle the Shadows," Zane told them, watching their looks of disbelief as they shook their heads. "The original crystals were created as a way of life for those born without powers and not in this realm. They were never meant to come to Earth." Telara stared at him, feeling frozen in her seat, it was as if he were repeating Kyler's words almost verbatim.

"They were brought here by a traitor," Telara filled in for him.

Turning towards her he watched her with great interest, something that put her on edge during her first days here but it seemed she was now getting used to it, even though she still didn't understand it. "I've heard that version but have also heard that they were brought here to heal, that upon healing they would go back to their realm where they belong."

"You got all that from the book I.Q. gave you?" Vanna asked him.

His lips quirked. "Some, yes but I have my other sources that tell me things as well."

"What sources?" Vanna shot back.

"Sources that would like to remain in the dark for now." He winked at her. "When they are ready to step into the light, I'll gladly introduce you."

"What about the Shadows?" Telara interrupted.

"What about them?" Zane looked at her.

"How will we be able to fight them without the crystals?" she asked him.

"The Shadows are nothing more than injured souls that will heal with the crystals, you would no longer need the crystals to keep the Shadows at bay," he told them.

"What about our powers?" Chad spoke up.

"You don't need crystals to work your powers," Zane told him. "You've proven that many times since you came here."

"What about the Arions in Sanctuary and all the outposts?" Tia stepped into the conversation.

"They could be kids once again, live a normal life," Zane told her. "Well, as normal as they can when they live among the magical creatures."

"So, we're destined to heal the crystals?" Telara brought his attention back to her, he nodded. "But how?"

"That I don't know." He reached for one of the chocolates. "The prophecy says you will heal the crystals but it doesn't say how it is to happen. That's the trouble with prophecies, they never give you all the information."

Telara snorted. "You're telling me."

"So, what is this?" I.Q. pointed to the Stargazer.

"Looks like a journal." Zane looked over at him. "Something you should be able to access with no problem."

"What do you mean?" They were all just as curious as I.Q. about that statement.

"With your powers, you should be able to link with the Stargazer, as you call it." Zane grinned and motioned towards the purplish shiny box. "Give it a try, command it to answer you."

They watched as I.Q. reached for the Stargazer and held it in his hands, staring intensely at the screen. The crackling sound of electricity started low, then gained in volume. They could see shards of electricity race across I.Q.'s skin, attaching to the Stargazer which came to life before them. "Who is your creator?" I.Q. stared at the screen where pictures started to flash of all of them until they were staring at Lucius, looking just like he did when they left Sanctuary. Rather than flash to another picture, his picture stayed there. I.Q. looked at them. "This journal belongs to Lucius."

CHAPTER 22

Staring up at the ceiling, Telara missed her little friends from her room back at Sanctuary. They always helped her to relax. Instead, she found herself wide awake thinking over the events from the day. She really wanted to know more about the prophecy Zane spoke about, that was the first she had ever heard about it. I.Q. leaving the Stargazer with him last night showed how much they had come to trust Zane in the short time they had known him.

A twinge of guilt peaked in her gut as she realized that while Zane was being open with them, she seemed to be holding back. Wasn't that her complaint about Lucius and the others at Sanctuary? Doesn't that make her a hypocrite? She tried reasoning with herself that she didn't know for sure that he was being completely open with them, but even in her own head that sounded hollow.

"How do you expect to get anything done when you keep obsessing over that which has already taken place and can't be undone?"

Telara looked around her, sure enough, she was no

longer in her bed but lounging on a chaise lounger that felt softer than any bed she had ever slept on. Royal blue with a seashell back and curled arm rests. There standing above her with that better than thou look was Kyler. She groaned, moving to stand up. They were in the room with the pictures of other realms covering the one side of the room, the swirling time travel portal on the back wall and the new addition of the chaise lounge.

"I don't remember falling asleep," she said, giving Kyler an accusatory look, one that bounced off the Crystal Keeper with no effect.

"You were taking too long."

Telara stared at her in amazement, "you can just pull me here, even when I'm not sleeping?"

"You're sleeping now."

Telara sighed and spoke slowly, wanting Kyler to understand each word that came out of her mouth. "Don't do that again."

"I don't have all day and neither do you," Kyler informed her, not even acknowledging her transgression. Of course, knowing Kyler, could be that she doesn't consider it a transgression.

"What do you mean?" Telara couldn't keep her irritation out of her voice, no matter how hard she tried. The only one who made sense in this new world of theirs was Zane, everyone else seemed to thrive on confusing her and she was really getting tired of it.

"When you wake up, everything will change."

"I'm lost." That was the last thing she expected Kyler to say to her. She felt some satisfaction when Kyler's expression showed confusion.

"You're right here."

She held back a chuckle. "No, I don't understand what you're talking about."

"Because you don't stop to listen."

Goodbye humor, hello aggravation. She took a deep breath. "I'm listening." Words spoken through stiff lips. Kyler raised a brow at the tone, so she attempted a calming breath. "I'm trying."

"You need to be ready for what's coming."

"And what is that?"

"Betrayal."

Telara wished hearing that was surprising to her. "That's about becoming the norm." She sighed, wondering which one of their new friends they met this summer was actually working for the Shadow Master. She had her money on Billy, his sister she was sure was on the right side though. Maybe Billie and Pam could start a support group. Ouch, that sounded mean.

"Not this one, this one will shake you to your core. But if you keep your head, you can use it, make it your saving grace."

"Seriously?" She was just getting past the part about it shaking her to her core when Kyler said to make it her saving grace. Was this woman mental? How do you make a betrayal your saving grace?

"Yes."

Telara was truly attempting to keep herself calm. "How do you know this?"

"It is written."

"Where? Where is all this written?" Kyler gave her a pointed look at the volume of her words, but she refused to apologize or even acknowledge it. She was tired of stupid riddles.

"It doesn't matter." Kyler's almost bored tone was like nails on a chalkboard.

"It does to me, this is my life!" Telara felt her eyes burn and her throat feel tight.

Kyler watched her. "You really want to know?"

Telara barely bit back the 'duh'. "Yes!"

"It is written in the crystals, if you learn to connect with them, they will speak to you as well."

"How?"

"When you don't have to ask, you will know."

"That's stupid!"

Kyler's eyes narrowed at her but before she could say anything else, she was laying back in her bed. She groaned, hitting her bed. "Sensitive dictator."

"Shayne's there?"

A scoff could be heard from the screen Billie was talking to. "Trying to act like queen of the court, as always."

"Stazi allows that?"

"Let's just say that Shayne was put with Trevor to go patrol the marshes," They could hear the malice in Lucy's voice.

"That will do wonders for her hair." Billie chuckled.

"Especially if Trevor does what he promised he would do."

Billie raised a brow. "Do I want to know?"

"Probably not."

Telara and the other Guardians were watching Billie chatting with Lucy via crystal screen; they had heard all about the deal with Shayne, Paul and Lucy when they were at the Hunter's headquarters. So, what they were hearing wasn't a surprise to them at all. They were all laughing when Billy charged into the building barking out orders to the Arions that were following him.

"Don't forget the illusion and memory crystals," he told a small dark-haired boy who was following him closely. When the kid took off to grab the crystals, Billy turned towards his sister. "Send out an all-hands alert, Shadows in Savana."

"Anything we can do?" Lucy spoke from the screen.

"Sure, have dinner and a bath ready for me when I get back."

Vanna's eyes widened as she looked at Billy, who wasn't paying them any attention, his relaxed Crim gripped in his hands.

"I'm not your servant, Billy." Lucy's droll voice shot back.

"Sure you are." Billy wasn't even looking at her as he spoke, moving to grab a crystal utility belt, just like the ones back at Sanctuary. Crystals of all uses attached as well as some bulging pockets full of crystals.

"I don't know how your girlfriend puts up with you." Lucy shook her head.

"Same reason you do, she loves me and she doesn't have a choice." Arrogance spoken in such a nonchalant way that it was spoken as if fact.

"I don't know how you get through those doorways with that big head," Lucy told him before looking towards Billie. "If you need anything, send me a line."

"Thanks, Lucy." Billie smiled as the crystal screen went blank. Grabbing her crystal pen on a chain she twirled the chain around her wrist, then let the pen dangle. Turning to her brother, "is Reggie and the others going to meet us there?"

Billy jerked his arm up, Crim held tightly in his hand; green crystal limbs grew from each end of the Crim in elegant arches that any elven cosplayer would be jealous of. The bow didn't have the epic look of I.Q.'s, the edges weren't as jagged, more rounded with a natural look, more regal. "Can't reach 'em." He looked over at Telara and the others who were watching. "Wanna play?"

No hesitation as I.Q. flicked his wrist, turning his watch into the jagged, epic bow of his. A green brow rose, signaling that the gesture wasn't lost on Billy. Walking to the back of the room where there were several crystal buttons along the wall, Billy placed his hand on the third one in. The wall started to glow as a doorway appeared, on the other side was trees with Spanish Moss draping down making a picturesque view. If it weren't for the Shadows running around causing panic with Georgians and tourists screaming in terror. Looking back at them. "What are you waiting for?" With those words he moved through the door followed by his sister and other Arions rushing through with utility belts around their waist.

They looked at each other and shrugged. "Guess we better move before the door shuts on us." Telara chuckled.

Tia snorted. "Which would end up being our fault, I'm pretty sure."

They moved through the doorway just as it started to shrink, the air around them hot and humid as the door disappeared and the cool air with it. They saw people placing illusion crystals all along the outside of the area they were in, a large square park with a street that ran around the outside of the square. A majestic fountain in the center with water cascading down. Buildings made of brick and mortar with black iron fences. Tia moved forward, jerking back as a long strand of Spanish Moss hit her in the face. Tia jerked away quickly, remembering Logan's remarks from their first day here.

Chad chuckled.

Tia glared at him. "Oh, shut it."

They were all grinning when a flash of greenish blue had Telara turning around quickly, frowning when she saw nothing but an empty sidewalk. "Sid you see that?" she asked the others.

"See what?" Vanna looked in the same direction. "I don't see anything."

"It was a flash of … a mermaid tail." Telara finished awkwardly.

"Mermaid tail?" Cole gave her a funny look.

"Well, it was the same color," she bit back defensively.

"Since when do all mermaids have the same color of tails?" I.Q. asked, which made her chuckle since the question came from him.

She gave a sigh. "The color the stores use when they are making mermaid things. Shiny greenish-blue, it was just a flash but I swear it was there." She looked around but couldn't see anything close to that.

"I didn't see anything," Tia said as the others nodded in agreement. Telara gave a disgruntled sigh then jerked as something big and fuzzy bopped her on the nose, almost making her sneeze. She swatted at it before rubbing her nose.

"What's this?" Vanna picked up the stick with the long slender stems sticking out from the top of the stick, white fluffs at the end of them. "This looks like a dande-lion seed."

"That's one huge dandelion," Cole said, reaching for the stick but Vanna swatted his hand away.

"Are you guys planning on joining or just going to play tourist?" Billy glared at them, raising his bow and shooting out an arrow of light that connected with the slithering shapeshifting Shadow who let out a scream, without even looking away from them to make sure he hit his mark.

"Whoa," Chance breathed, reaching to his ear to pull down the water flail.

Cole gulped as he pulled down his necklace that transformed into his fiery nunchucks in his hands. "Maybe we should shelve this conversation until after we have dispatched the Shadows."

Billy snorted. "Grand idea." Then he muttered something about kids attempting to play heroes until it cuts into their playtime.

Vanna stuffed the dandelion seed into her back pocket, pulled off her belt that straightened out into her elegant staff. "Let's show him our version of playtime." She gave Billy a haughty look, even though he wasn't looking their way at all and headed towards the battle taking place in the square.

"We'll figure out what you saw later, Telly," Tia promised her, holding the whip that had once been her arm band. The whip that was already creating gusts of winds.

Chad was twirling his icy sword, moving forward with them. "Let's send these Shadows back to the darkness where they came from."

Telara grinned, her Rotary starting to glow as they moved forward. "Sounds like a plan to me."

CHAPTER 23

Telara raised her arm, her Rotary created a force shield that deflected the assault of an aggressive Shadow bear that charged her. The force from the assault had her falling back, throwing out her hand behind her she created another force field that kept her straight up. Flipping backwards she used her power to vault her even farther from the reach of the Shadow who was once again attempting to catch her. A mighty gust of wind knocked the bear off his hind legs. Telara turned to see Tia holding out her hand towards the fallen bear, the gusts had died down but her whip was taking out a feline Shadow that was vaulting towards her with one swift crack!

More snapping sounds could be heard as I.Q. let his electric arrows fly towards the shapeshifting Shadows.

"Careful dammit!" Billy shouted at I.Q.. "You almost hit crazy Mary."

They looked at him frowning, "Who?" I.Q. asked, lowering his bow with a quizzical expression looking around. They saw Billie and a few other Arions rushing towards what they thought was a garbage can next to a wooden bench. As they watched, the top of the garbage can lifted up and they saw a bedraggled older woman staring up at Billie.

Vanna looked over at Billy. "Shouldn't you be using the memory crystals on her and getting her out of the way?"

"Sure." Se snorted. "We would gladly do that if the crystals would work on her." He shot an arrow up into the air, it exploded above them lighting up the area as Shadows let out wails trying to hide from the bright light.

"They don't work on her?" Tia stared at him with a surprised expression before looking back at Crazy Mary who was looking around her as if she wasn't comprehending what was going on.

Billy shook his head. "The crystals go wonky whenever they get near her."

"Could she be a Shadow?" I.Q. looked at her with interest, they looked at Billy to hear his response.

Billy leveled them with one of his signature "you're an idiot and you know nothing" glowering looks.

"What?" Chance stepped forward. "It's an honest question."

Billy turned his hard stare onto Chance. "You don't think we wouldn't guess that and make sure?"

"Maybe…" Chad spoke in a small voice, looking down.

Billie rolled her eyes as she moved Crazy Mary from the bench, closer to where the Guardians were standing under the trees. "She is no Shadow. Crystals don't work on her but it doesn't matter."

"It doesn't?" Telara raised a brow looking at Billie.

"No, she doesn't know what is going on around her."

Billie pulled the hood back from Crazy Mary's face and they could see that she wore a blank expression. Her mouth was moving, but no sound was coming out as her eyes stared straight through them. Billie put the hood back over her head as she moved away from an exasperated Billie.

"The biggest problem," Billy cocked an arrow and let it fly, "is keeping her safe." A slithering, Shadow-like snake that was nearing Crazy Mary let out a pained scream, writhing.

"I can see how that would be," I.Q. let one of his electric arrows fly, the Shadow disappeared upon impact, "aggravating." Billy's scowl had them all looking away except for I.Q. who was grinning unapologetically.

"Just be careful and don't hurt Mary, or you'll deal with me." That wiped the smile off I.Q.'s face. "Let's move."

Billie gave a shake of her head, muttering something about too much testosterone and not enough action to back it up. The guys all gave wounded looks while her brother just glowered at her. The girls barely held back their snickers as they moved forward with Billie who was advancing on the Shadows with her glowing pen lasso, keeping Mary behind them.

"Welcome to Savanna historic district," one of the Arions that were moving along with them told them wryly. "One of the hottest tourist spots."

"How often do Shadows attack here?" Water droplets sprinkled the area as Chance twirled his flail around.

Billie shrugged. "We don't keep tallies, we just work to keep our part of the world safe."

"Why are they attacking here?" Telara looked around, her brow furrowing as she noticed the Shadows weren't rushing them. Several of them were hanging around the fountain while others were hanging back watching them. "What is here that they want?"

"Like they need to have a reason?" Billy snorted.

"Even mindless, soulless creatures have purpose." Air flew around them from the whip that was swirling around Tia as she walked, she was watching the Shadows with the same curiosity.

"You've never seen a Shadow attack for no reason?" Billie spared barely a glance their way.

"Honestly," I.Q. joined the conversation, looking around them carefully as they moved, "the only nonsensical attack that didn't have a reason was the first battle in Texas, and even that one they ended up capturing an Arion. These don't seem to be interested in any of us," he finished, his fingers worrying the electric string.

"Any magic that you know of in the square?" Vanna twirled her staff, turning when she saw some Shadows attempt to move past them to Mary who was stumbling around behind them with no true destination.

"The only magic is the history of the square," Logan spoke from behind them, startling them all as they jerked around staring at him.

Billy glowered at him. "Where have you been?"

Logan shrugged, twirling the crystal spear in his hand. "Everyone was gone when I got back from patrols, if I hadn't gone through the call log and contacted Lucy, I wouldn't have known what was going on." He twirled in place. "So here I am."

"Can you tell us why the Shadows are acting strangely?" Tia looked over at him, her whip still moving around her body.

Logan looked over towards the Shadows then let his gaze run over the square, resting briefly on Mary who was running her fingers down a vine of Spanish Moss, her lips moving although whatever she was saying they couldn't hear. Looking back at them. "They haven't attacked?"

"They were attacking until we got Mary out of the way." Chad looked from the Shadows to Mary who was now stumbling away from the tree towards them, back to the Shadows. "You don't think they could be after her?"

"She has been here for as long as I can remember," Billie told them, watching Mary and the Shadows as well. "If they were after her, they had many chances."

"Maybe they have tried before." Telara looked at Billy. "You said you've had to try to keep the Shadows off of her when fighting before, maybe she was their goal."

He frowned at her, looking towards Mary, who stumbled over a crack in the sidewalk, the Shadow's attention was moved from them to her as she moved away from the Arions and Guardians. Vanna vaulted over them, bringing her staff down onto the sidewalk, sending green leafy vines slithering out from the staff towards the Shadows who tried to flee from them but failed as their bodies were wrapped tightly. The leafy cocooned bodies started to glow brightly, muffled screams could be heard before the cocoons deflated like a popped balloon and slithered back to the staff. Standing back up she stared at the Shadows who were watching from around the fountain.

"Watch out!" Telara moved to intercept Mary, who suddenly lunged at Vanna's back but she was flung back by her own Rotary. "Oomph!" She landed hard on the ground looking up at Mary who was holding the large dandelion seed in her hand. Around her were the other Guardians, Billie and her brother who must have tried to intercept Mary as well. Vanna was the closest to Mary, her body awkwardly on the rough sidewalk, watching the seed start to glow brightly. The glow moved from the seed down Mary's arm until it encased her entire body.

Telara jumped up, crouched on the ground, her arm out in front of her with her Rotary glowing as they waited to see what was happening. So focused on Mary they had forgotten all about the Shadows that were still in the square. A tentacle wrapped around Telara's chest, yanking her back with a shriek. She raised her arm, creating a glowing spike to stab the tentacle but before she could, the tentacle lifted her up and slammed her back on the ground, knocking the breath out of her.

Around her the Shadows were attacking the others who weren't expecting the assault either, Cole was wrestling a massive Shadow bear who knocked his nunchucks from his grasp right before striking him with one of the beefy paws, knocking him sideways onto the sidewalk. Billy and I.Q. were standing back-to-back shooting light and electric arrows at a swarm of flying Shadows that were dive-bombing them. It was almost impossible to decipher who was Shadows and who was Billy or I.Q. fighting. Chance was fighting snakes and gigantic spiders that sent shudders down Telara's spine along with Billie. His flail would hit one only to have another attack from another side. Billie stabbed one of the gigantic Spiders with the glowing pen only to get tossed away by a snake that had wrapped around her leg.

They weren't the only ones in peril. Tia, Vanna and Logan were being pelted by insect like Shadows that were attacking them from all sides even with Tia's glowing whip swirling around them. The flying Shadows seemed to be able to avoid the whip no matter how erratic it moved; Vanna's staff sliced through the air but for every dozen she knocked out of the sky three dozen would appear attacking them all. Logan's spear was having the same problem.

Ice shards were on the ground around Chad who was wrestling a feline Shadow that swiped at him with his sharp and dangerous claws. Telara was attempting to keep her focus as black spots started to dance in front of her, the tentacles around her chest squeezing tighter. She was not letting them take away her power like they did in Illinois. She closed her eyes and imagined the air around her expanding, pushing out the tentacles even as she gasped for breath. Some relief came when the tentacles around her chest seemed to loosen, she squirmed away and rolled away from the mass of tentacles that were actually an octopus. "Stupid ass Shadows, don't you know that water creatures can't breathe on land," she muttered as she attempted to push herself from the ground.

Before she could rise to help her friends when the sound of gurgling water could be heard, she looked up and saw water from the fountain overflow over the sides and rush towards them. She looked over at Chance but he was still battling the Shadow snakes, so no way was this his doing. She tensed as the water started to move their way, looking anywhere to see where the water was coming from but all Arions and her fellow Guardians were still engaged in battle with the Shadows. She felt the slimy tentacle wrap around her ankle moments before she hit the ground again. Pushing herself up she brought down her Rotary that had formed into a blade, onto the Shadow tentacle effectively slicing into it. The shriek was painful as she flipped backwards, landing on her feet, her arm held out in front of her, waiting for the Shadow's attack that never came.

The water from the fountain had reached them all but instead of engulfing everyone the water encased all the Shadows, releasing the fighters from the Shadow's clutches. They all moved quickly from the water encased Shadows that were floundering about.

"What is going on?" I.Q. looked at Telara but she had no answer as she stared. A gasp had them looking at Vanna, they turned to look where she was pointing.

Telara stumbled back as she stared at the two females standing there, dark black skin, silver hair with purple and blue hues, one with blue eyes and one with purple eyes. While Telara stared at them they weren't even paying any of them any mind. A crackling sound had them all turning to see streaks of electricity moving through the water, heading straight for all the Shadows. The square lit up with flashing lights when the electricity reached all the Shadows whose mouths were open in silent screams. The Shadows exploded in bursts of water and sparks all around them, soaking them all, even Chance who was too stunned to deflect the water.

CHAPTER 24

K ala! Kali!"
Both of them turned to look at Telara who was staring at them, they looked pleased to see her. "Tien."

"Uh, no." Telara gave a slight shake of her head. "Telara."

Both the women turned to look at her, their heads cocked slightly in the same manner, but it was the one with blue eyes who spoke. "No, that isn't who you are." She reached out and ran her fingers down Telara's cheek. "I worried I would never see you again." She looked around at everyone standing there staring at them. "Worried we wouldn't see any of you again. I'm glad to see we were wrong."

"Who are you?" Billy crossed his arms, giving them a hard stare.

They looked over at him and some of the other Arions. "You all have the air of magic about you, but you are not our descendants."

Billy frowned, looking between the Guardians and the two Paladins standing there. "What the hell does that have to do with me asking who you are?"

A shimmering blue brow raised thoughtfully before turning to look at her sister. "Could he be some distant relative of Kull's?"

Vanna, Tia, Chad, Chance, I.Q. and Telara each let out a quickly suppressed snort of laughter while Cole just gave a disgruntled look. Billy frowned at them but that did nothing but cause snickers. "We need to get back to Haven and let Zane know what's going on, this could have something to do with the disappearances."

"Zane?" Kali asked sharply, looking at Billy, her blue eyes narrowing. "Did you just say Zane?"

Billy frowned at her. "He is the commander of the Haven outpost of Sanctuary."

Kali turned to Telara and the others. "Tell me you haven't been working with him."

"Zane?" Telara frowned at her. "Why wouldn't we? He's the only one who hasn't lied to us."

"Oh really?" Kala asked. "Did he tell you that he was the one who brought the Shadows to this realm?"

Telara felt as if the ground beneath her had disappeared and she was falling through an endless vortex. "He's the Shadow Master?" She turned to the others, feeling her eyes tear up; she saw their astonished looks as well.

"I know nothing about this Shadow Master, what I know is that he brought the Shadows here," Kala told them gently, "and you shouldn't trust him."

Telara shook her head. "I don't believe you; he isn't the Shadow Master."

Billie moved forward. "Let's get back to Haven, we can ask him and get his side." She gave Kala and Kali a hard stare that mirrored her brothers, "he has been our leader our whole life, we just met you two and while you have been masquerading as Crazy Mary, he has been our mentor. You want us to believe that he is our enemy that we've been fighting our whole life? That isn't possible."

"We will ask him," Billy told them.

"I would love to talk to him," Kala informed her. "He has a lot to answer for, disappearances of our family and the curse that kept me and my sister unable to communicate with anyone."

"Keep in mind that he is our mentor, you're not," Logan told her, his jovial tone they were used to seeing gone and his expression unwelcome. Not that they blamed him, they weren't feeling very charitable to these two, even if they had been cursed. He held out a silver remote, pushing a button. He stared in front of him but nothing happened, he frowned pushing the button again but still nothing. He looked at Billy who held out his own remote pushing a button, getting the same results. They looked at each other with mirrored expressions of anxiety.

The twins frowned, "was something supposed to happen?" Kali asked them.

"Yeah, a doorway should've appeared to Haven," Billie told them, looking between Logan and her brother as several of the Arions around them started to look nervous. "How are we going to get back there?" she asked her brother.

Telara looked at Vanna who was looking down at the ground. "Van, think you can do it?"

"Do what?" Billy looked between them all, but his sister turned to look at them, her eyes lighting up as she remembered the battle at the borders of Haven.

"Can she move all of us?" she asked.

"I'm standing right here." Vanna crossed her arms, giving Billie a dark look.

"Uh…sorry." Billie pressed her lips together. "Can you move all of us?" She gestured around the square.

Vanna looked around them and gave a shake of her head. "I doubt I can move everyone here but I can attempt to get most of us, the others will have to find their own ride." She took a deep breath moving forward standing in the grass and closing her eyes. The ground rumbled beneath them, they all put out their hands as if to steady themselves on some unseen surface. Telara looked down and saw a large green leaf grow from the ground around them, growing until it encased them completely. Vanna's eyes were still closed as they felt the leaf sink into the ground with them in its embrace. They fell to their knees when the leaf jerked before speeding through the ground.

Telara looked around at everyone, "we don't know what we're heading into, so we better be prepared. I would keep your Crims at the ready." Everyone nodded in agreement as they felt the leaf rising through the ground until it broke through the surface, the leaf folding back to release them into Haven where they saw Zane standing with Reggie, Pam and Flint. Telara's stomach dropped at what else they saw, all around Haven were Shadows of different sizes but all looked menacing as they watched them. They were on top of the pillars surrounding the coliseum, on top of the stables which were making the equestrians inside titter nervously, on top of the hills where the different barracks resided and standing alongside Zane, Reggie, Pam and Flint as well as the other Arions who were standing behind Zane and them. Shapeshifting Shadows, Minion Shadows, as well as Generals that were of a bigger stature.

Telara shook her head as she looked all around them, not believing what she was seeing. She could feel the same confusion radiating from the others, looking over at Billy, Billie and Logan she saw rigid profiles as they stared at their commander. Their faces white, lips pressed together as well as fists clenched at their sides.

She looked back at Zane who was smiling, SMILING, at her. She opened her mouth to ask … she didn't know what to ask. She knew what it looked like, but it couldn't be. Why was he standing with the Shadows? Why was Pam standing next to her brother? Were they all working for the Shadow Master?

Zane looked over at Vanna and told her, "I'm proud of how well you have mastered your powers, I truly didn't expect you guys to arrive back so quickly without the use of the crystal doors." He spoke as if they were sitting in his office talking about their powers and not in the middle of Haven with Shadows all around them as well as a known traitor. He looked over at Telara and gave her one of his proud smiles.

"No." Telara shook her head then looked around them. "What's going on?" She looked over at Pam, whose expression was full of guilt and sorrow. "Pam, what are you doing?" When Pam opened her mouth to respond, Flint put his hand on her shoulder in support.

"You don't owe them an explanation, sis," Flint told her.

"Yes, she does!" Telara practically screamed, her voice almost breaking with emotion as she attempted to comprehend what was happening. Denying what was obvious and praying it was anything but.

Flint stared at her. "No, she doesn't. You don't get to make her choose between friendship and family."

"What about your other family?" Telara moved forward aggressively, several of the Shapeshifting Shadows that had the forms of felines as well as bears moved forward as if ready to stop her if she were to get closer to Zane and the others. She looked at Zane. "What are you doing? You're supposed to be the good guy."

"I am the good guy," he told her. He turned to look at Kali when she snorted. "What do you know of it?"

"I know you're the one who cursed us!" she accused him.

It was his turn to snort. "I never cursed you; I don't even have that ability."

"No, but your buddies the Greek Gods you claimed to have no use for sure do," she shot right back at him.

He leveled her with a hard stare. "You know nothing about what I've been through, what truly happened or who started all this."

"So, why don't you educate me?" She practically sneered at him.

"Enough." He turned to Reggie, Flint, Pam and the other Arions standing behind him. Raising his hand, a dark swirling portal of shadows appeared behind them all. "Go, I'll join you shortly." After shooting them a pained look, Pam walked through the portal with her brother and the others. Zane turned back, this time he addressed I.Q. who hadn't said a word since they arrived. He tossed not only the book I.Q. had loaned him but the Stargazer as well, Telara had forgotten about them loaning him those. "I want to thank you for the reads, they are both pretty interesting. You should finish deciphering them, there was some information in them even I didn't know."

Telara's throat felt tight as she implored him. "You could help with that."

The smile Zane gave her at her words sparked a tiny flame of hope within her, one that was quickly dashed with his words. "Come with me and I will."

It felt as if the breath had been knocked from her lungs, her chest hurt, each breath she breathed in felt as if took all her strength.

"Telly." Looking over at Tia, who wore a concerned expression, she realized she hadn't responded to Zane. She wanted to say that it was because she was stunned by what was happening, but the reality was that she was actually considering his offer. Closing her eyes, she breathed in slowly and turned to Zane whose smile had already lost some of its shine.

"I know," he told her sadly. "You can't."

She knew she was being watched closely by everyone, she didn't care, all she cared about was that two people she had trusted were now her enemies and she didn't like it. "I trusted you, I trusted Pam." Her voice quivered. "We finally had someone that we believed who wasn't lying to us."

"I never lied to you," he protested. "I never will."

She shook her head incredulously at him. "You lied about the most important part, about who you truly are."

"I might have not have told you who I am, but I never lied," he said. "There is so much you don't know and my offer to tell you everything still stands." He held out a hand. "All you have to do is come with me, I won't hold anything back, I promise."

Telara stared at his hand as the urge to do just that rode her hard, she could feel the distress from her friends because of the inner struggle she was facing. She knew they wouldn't stop her if she chose to join Zane, even though they felt it was a wrong decision. She let out a sigh, "the worst part about this is that I really wish I could," she heard the astonished gasps from the Arions around her but she didn't really care, nor did she care about the sharp looks that were being sent her way by Kali and Kala. "You're the enemy." This time tears did escape down her cheeks. "That isn't something I can just ignore."

"I understand," he spoke, his words full of emotion that seemed to mirror hers. He looked over at I.Q.. "There is a section in the Stargazer that tells of a prophecy about all of you, it tells you the truth about the past, if you can read between the lines." I.Q. looked down at the Stargazer then back up at Zane whose expression was full of regret but none of them knew exactly what it was he regretted. "If you truly want to know what happened, if you want to stop the past from repeating itself, translate it all." I.Q. stared at him silently, not sure what else to do or say.

His kind words, his caring manner, became too much for Telara who burst out, "Why do you even care about us? Why did you show us what we're truly capable of if you're just going to try to kill us?"

"I don't want to kill you," he told her firmly.

"Then what do you want?" She stared at him.

"I'm not sure you're ready to know," he said with sorrow, watching her.

"Why don't you let me be the judge of that," she countered and his lips twitched a bit.

"You have a lot of your mother in you." His words contained a bit of amusement even if they confused her.

"You act as if you're innocent but we saw you over Marsella's body/" Kali moved forward and the air around them started to crackle with her power. "We saw you and the Shadows."

"You don't know what you saw." His voice turned cold as he looked at them. "You never stopped to ask, did you?"

"We didn't need to ask, not after what you did to our family and friends!" Kala rose up on a wave that she conjured from beneath her. They both moved towards him but the Shadows moved quicker as they engulfed him, just as the wave crashed down on the spot where he had stood. When the Shadows dissipated, they saw that they were gone, along with Zane.

"You okay, Telly?" Tia looked at her, she swallowed hard before giving a nod.

"I think it's time Lucius answered our questions," she told them tightly, feeling as if she was completely numb inside, they all nodded in agreement with her. The fact that she had considered joining the Shadow Master only moments before not spoken of.

CHAPTER 25

Y ou guys ready to come home?" Lucius smiled at them from the crystal screen they were using at Billie's desk. It was only one day since they discovered the identity of the Shadow master, Telara wanted to call Lucius immediately but Tia convinced her to wait a day. They needed to rest and help their new friends in Haven with getting their home back up and running. Logan was next in line but he declined saying he wasn't a leader, so by unanimous vote, Billy was the new leader of Haven. Unless Sanctuary decided to intervene but they were pretty sure that Sanctuary was going to have enough to do without worrying who was running Haven right now. The twins, Kali and Kala, had already left but promised they would see them soon.

"Yes," Telara told him. "Grandfather." They watched as his face went completely white, he didn't bother to deny it, this time he was the one who looked as if he was at a loss for words. "Billie is going to set up one of their crystal doors to Sanctuary and when we get home, I think it's time for a long conversation."

Lucius nodded. "I agree."

"Full disclosure this time," I.Q. put in.

Lucius gave another nod. "Full disclosure," he agreed.

Telara looked back at them as the screen went black. "Ready to go home?" Everyone inclined their heads in agreement.

Lucius stared at the blank screen in front of him, for the first time in his long life, he felt light. As if a mighty weight had been lifted. He chuckled as he leaned back, "about time, I'm ready for things to finally come out in the open."

"You may be ready for that, but I'm not." The ominous tone from the doorway had him turning swiftly to see Hades standing there with a scowl on his face.

Lucius chuckled. "Then you might want to get ready, threaten all you want, Hades. These Guardians are more than enough for you and your threats."

"Only if they have all the information," Lucius narrowed his eyes at the implied threat in Hades' words.

"You can't stop me from telling them everything I know." Lucious stood up to stare at the God.

"Don't be too sure of that," Hades told him.

"Lucius!"

They both turned to see Ira down the hallway, rushing towards them, the sly smile on Hades' face was the only warning Lucius had before the God of the Underworld shimmered them from his office in a puff of smoke. "It's Hades, Ira!" Lucius shouted as the world around him went dark.

"Lucius!" Ira's startled shout followed them.

Ira stared at the spot behind Lucius' big oak desk

where only moments Lucius had stood with Hades, Ira had never seen a God or Goddess, never expected to honestly but this surely wasn't how he expected it to happen. He looked around him, he needed to talk to the leaders.

It took more time than he wanted to reach the Command Center, so he headed straight to his office where his assistant, Kristin, was at her desk rifling through papers as he entered. "I need to speak to Leaders, Kristin."

She raised a single white brow at that. "Then shouldn't you talk to Lucius?" she asked him as she continued to peruse the papers in the file.

"Hades kidnapped him, Kristin," Ira told her impatiently. "I need to let the Leaders know."

She stared up at him with wide eyes, her hands going still. "That isn't good."

"Exactly," he told her, reaching for a bunch of crystals on small chains from a drawer in his desk. "If anyone comes looking for me, tell them I'm unavailable for the time being." She inclined her head, her white spiky hair bobbing as she watched him rush off. Standing calmly, she shut his door and returned to her desk where she went back to the file sitting there.

Ira was standing in the middle of the empty room, no desks, no window and only one door. He had never before spoken to the Leaders, his predecessor had told him to only use those crystal keys in the case of an emergency, lest he anger the Leaders. Only the Caretaker was to converse with the Leaders, well the God of the Underworld kidnapping the Caretaker constituted an emergency in his book.

"What business do you have with us, Commander of the Command Center?"

Ira twisted around and saw several silhouettes on the walls around him, they were of all different sizes with no exact form. Looking around he thought one silhouette had wings, one had two big pillars behind them, one looked to be small in stature while another seemed to stand tall, another's head seemed to be quite large and then one looked to be a standard silhouette of male.

"Commander?" The voice from earlier sounded sharper to get his attention.

"Yes." Ira straightened. "I need to report that Lucious has been kidnapped by Hades." When the silhouettes said nothing, not even moved, he continued, "We need to discuss the Guardians."

"What is there to discuss?" The more feminine voice spoke.

"It has been discovered that the Leader of Haven is the Shadow Master, he has left and taken more of our Arions with him," Ira said, when he got no reactions he continued, "with this new development I believe that the Guardians should stay at Sanctuary and not return to their homes in the mortal world."

"The Guardians will continue as Lucius has wanted," the commanding voice that spoke at the beginning informed him.

"But Lucius is no longer here," Ira protested but a hand was raised to stop him.

"That matters not," he was informed, to his aggravation.

Arriving at Sanctuary, Telara and the other Guardians rushed towards the bungalow, making a beeline for Lucious' office. "Where is he?" I.Q. looked over at Telara who was shaking her head as she backed away. "Telara?" She gave a shake of her head and turned, running out of the bungalow.

"Telara!" Tia shouted after her but she didn't stop. Tia looked at the others and sighed. "We better go find her, no telling what trouble she could get into without us." They all nodded as they took off after Telara.

They caught up with Telara who was talking to a smaller woman with white spiky hair, sitting behind a desk outside of Ira's office. They had never been there but Ira's name was there on the door. Telara turned around when they got there. "Hades kidnapped Lucius and now Ira is speaking with the Leaders."

"The same Leaders that only speak to Lucius?" I.Q. queried but the woman behind the desk didn't bother to respond to him. "So, how do we find them?"

"If you kids will excuse me." Kirstin stood up and moved around her desk. "I have some errands that need to get done." Giving them a slight nod, she walked past them.

I.Q. looked at Telara, who grinned as she held up a crystal on a chain. "What's that?" he asked her.

"The key!" Telara grinned and they moved down the hallway.

"You know where we're going right?" Chad looked around them as they followed her.

"Yup." Telara turned down a side hallway moving down a long corridor that seemed to go forever, away from the Command Center. "Seems reading minds comes easy when you just don't care." She shrugged as they turned to go down another hallway. At the end of the hallway Telara held up the crystal, the door opened and there stood Ira speaking to the silhouettes. Ira looked at them in shock, he definitely didn't expect to see them. "We have some questions." They moved into the room.

"Guardians!" the tallest silhouette acknowledged them.

"We need to rescue Lucius," Cole told them. "Hades has him."

"We are aware that Lucius has been taken by Hades," the male spoke.

"What are we going to do about it?" Telara asked them.

"You will do nothing," a feminine voice spoke to them. "You will go home for your senior year, train as you have been doing and return back to Sanctuary for the final time after you graduate."

"What do you mean, final time?" Telara asked them, everyone else just as curious.

"Lucius granted the Guardians time with their families until they graduated, after graduation they are to leave their families and return to Sanctuary where they will prepare for the final battle with the Shadow Master and his Magine." Another of the feminine silhouettes spoke.

"What about our families?" Chance asked, his blood going cold, a feeling they shared.

"They won't remember you after you leave," the voice told them. "That will be taken care of."

"What do you mean you will take care of that?" Telara asked them, looking around, her chest tightening.

"What are you going to do to our families?"

Telara shook her head as she felt more tightening in her chest. "You can't just take us away from our families." She looked at the others, whose expressions mirrored hers.

Ira sighed. "I know Lucius thought he was being kind but what is more cruel? Never having family or friends or having them only to have to say goodbye to them." He looks at her, "you and your friends have made many friends here who have come to care for you. They have even been attempting to find a way to alter your fate." Ira laughed at their surprised looks. "Think I didn't know? How will those friends feel when you're gone?" Telara stared at him feeling as if she were having an out of body experience, on the outside looking in. She had never thought about the feelings of the friends they had made during their time here in Sanctuary, those whose memories wouldn't be wiped. "Hard and cruel yes, but still the truth." Ira turned away and walked out of the room. "Don't worry about your training this year, spend as much time with your family as you can."

The fact that Ira was being kind to them added to their unreal feeling of what was happening around them, none of this felt real. Telara walked out of the room, the others following her but no one speaking. They could feel the maelstrom that was building within Telara and her inability to handle all the feelings that she was experiencing.

Telara didn't know where she was going, she didn't know what she was going to do, she didn't even know who to trust anymore. All she knew was that she was hurting. She came to a stop, looked around her and realized she was standing in the training room at Sanctuary. The same room where they worked out with Pam and the other Alphas. Where they started out hating each other and ended up working together as a team after they became friends.

Thinking of Pam brought more tightening to Telara's entire body as she thought about Pam leaving with Flint to join Zane, the Shadow Master. She trusted them, she had come to care for them both and they both betrayed her. Betrayed everyone. Her vision started to dim, her breathing coming in short gasps as her body tightened. She fell to her knees as tears cascaded down her cheeks, the roaring in her ears getting louder until she threw back her head and let out all her emotions out with a long blood curdling scream. The world around her exploded as her power released a vortex wave that cascaded out from her sweeping across the whole room.

Chad created an ice wall around them that exploded in millions of ice shards but at least protected them from the initial wave. They rushed to her side and wrapped their arms around her as she cried, feeling as if nothing was right within their world. Now it was truly only them.

CHAPTER 26

Y ou're distracted by the girl."

Zane was staring into the black fire crackling in the fireplace in his room, images dancing between the flames of Telara and her friends. He watched as her power exploded around her in her grief, he also saw something that no one else in the room saw, small Shadows that materialized before evaporating like smoke. He barely acknowledged the cloaked woman who entered his room as he watched the other Guardians try to comfort their leader and friend.

Looking down at the crystal prism in his palm, the blackness swirling with the white, clear and silver inside. Closing his fingers around the crystal he turned to her. "My… distractions …are none of your concerns."

Her eyes narrowed at him. "They are if they interfere with our goal, you haven't forgotten that have you?"

He stood and took a menacing step towards her but she held her ground as he stood before her, staring down at her. "I haven't forgotten my goal, woman, have you forgotten that you work for me?" The air around them darkened as menacing figures moved along the walls, the woman's eyes darted towards those figures as she stepped back, inclining her head slightly.

"Of course not, Zane, but we wouldn't want anything to hinder you from your final objective." With those words, she bowed her head and left the room, leaving Zane staring at the closed door with a furrowed brow.

"Nobody or nothing will stop me from my objective," his words were softly spoken but they were spoken firmly, even if he was the only one in the room. He moved to the table by his chair, to the pad of paper sitting there with the words written, words he had taken from the Stargazer as the Guardians called it. Lucius wrote everything he knew in there, everything Serdita had told him and all of his research. His father kept meticulous notes, something he had always been very adept at. Now, he hoped those notes would help him to reunite with his child and wife.

Only in darkness will you find the light
Only in the wrong will you find the right
Only in defeat will you be able to win
Only at the end will it all begin.

ABOUT THE AUTHOR

TL Shively is an award-winning author who loves her husband and three boys; they are not only a lot of her inspiration but also her greatest supporters. She is very outnumbered in a house full of boys; even their dog is male.

Her whole life has been full of stories that used to be only in her head, entertaining her when she was younger and lived in the country where the nearest neighbor was miles down the road. It wasn't until she was much older that she finally put these stories down on paper, and it was the Sanctuary Guardian's story that came out.

She loves anything fantasy: gaming, reading, writing, knick-knacks, you name it. She loves crafting of almost any kind and comes from a very artistic family.